JUDITH'S PLACE

Dreams of Plain Daughters, Book Two

By Diane Craver

Copyright 2013 by Diane Craver
All Rights Reserved

Editing by Regina Andrews

Judith's Place is a work of fiction. Though some actual towns, cities, and locations may be mentioned, they are used in a fictitious manner and the events and occurrences were invented in the mind and imagination of the author. Any similarities of characters or names used within to any person past, present, or future is coincidental.

All rights reserved. No part of this book may be used or reproduced in any manner whatsoever without written permission from the author. Brief quotations may be embodied in critical articles or reviews.

Reference: 'Scripture taken from the HOLY BIBLE, NEW INTERNATIONAL VERSION. Copyright 1973, 1978, 1984 by International Bible Society. Used by permission of Zondervan Publishing House', per the notice of copyright at the beginning of the Bible.

Scripture taken from the King James Version ®. © 1976 by Thomas Nelson, Inc., Nashville, TN. No permission listing is necessary as it's in the public domain per their website: thomasnelson.com/consumer/dept.asp?dept_id=190620&TopLevel_id=190000#KJV

To my amazing and beautiful daughter,
Christina. You're a wonderful blessing to me!

ACKNOWLEDGEMENTS

To my husband, Tom: I give thanks to God daily for you. You've always been supportive of my writing career, but most important to me is you're a loving Christian husband, father and grandfather.

To my children, Sara, Christina, April, Bartholomew, Emily and Amanda: You were the delight of my heart when you were my babies and through childhood. Now that you all are wonderful adult children, my blessings continue!

To my daughter-in-law, Lea and little grandson, Dillon: You both bring lots of love and happiness to the Craver family. Lea, my mother would have loved that you're a nurse. One of her desires was to have a nurse in the family, so I'm sure she's smiling down from heaven that now there finally is one!

To my friend, Michael Smith: Thank you for always taking the time through the years to fix my computers for me. From my first computer to the present, I've counted on your amazing technical knowledge, so I can continue to create my stories without having to resort to paper and pen!

To my editor, Regina Andrews: Thank you for your brilliant editing and unwavering support. Your suggestions helped me write the best book possible!

NOTE TO THE READER

The Amish community I've created is fictional, but exists close to Wheat Ridge which is an actual Amish community in the southern part of Ohio where I live. Before I started writing my Amish novel, I did extensive research to portray this wonderful faith as accurately as possible. I've used many rules and traditions common to the Amish way of life. However, there are differences between the various groups and subgroups of Amish communities. This is because the Amish have no central church government; each has its own governing authority. Every local church maintains an individual set of rules, adhering to its own *Ordnung*.

If you live near an Amish community, actions and dialogue in my book may differ from the Amish culture you know.

Pennsylvania Dutch Glossary

Aenti: aunt

boppli: baby

bopplin: babies

bruder: brother

daed: dad

danki: thank you

dat: father

Dietsch: Pennsylvania Dutch

dippy: term for easy over eggs

dochdern: daughters

ehemann: husband

eiferich: excited

English/Englischer: not Amish

fraa: wife

freinden: friends

froh: happy

frolic: a time for adult sisters to get together to visit with each other while doing chores such as canning food, cleaning house and more.

gegisch: silly

Gut nacht: Good night

Grossdaadi Haus: a smaller house that is connected to or nearby the main house, much like an "in-law suite"

grandkind: grandchild

grandkinner: grandchildren

grossdochdern: granddaughters

grossdaddi: grandfather

grossmammi: grandmother

gudemariye: good morning

gut: good

in lieb: in love

kaffi: coffee

kapp: prayer covering

kind: child

kinner: children

mamm: mom

naerfich: nervous

onkel: uncle

Ordnung: Set of rules for Amish and Old Order Mennonite living.

rumspringa or rumschpringe: running around; time before an Amish young person officially joined the church, provides a bridge between childhood and adulthood.

schweschder: sister

scholars: The Amish teachers call their students scholars.

wunderbaar: wonderful

ya: yes

Chapter One

Judith Hershberger had a few moments of quiet while the scholars played games during recess. She liked their daily schedule with one hour for lunch and recess. They also had a fifteen-minute break in the mid-morning and mid-afternoon. She was grateful for the weather being sunny and no wind so they could be outdoors on this January day. The temperature would drop considerably tomorrow to single digits so she and Ruth would keep them inside. Fortunately, they had a basement where they could release some energy playing Ping-Pong or board games when stuck inside for recess.

From her desk she could see that the the older children played softball while her younger ones had happy faces playing tag. *I love teaching the first four grades, especially teaching English to the first graders, but it'd be nice at some time in the future to teach the upper grades. More of a challenge.* Ruth Yoder taught fifth through eighth grade, and she didn't see that changing anytime in the future. Unless Ruth should get married which didn't look promising. At age thirty-five, Ruth never mentioned wanting to get married. She learned the sad story of Ruth's fiancé, Daniel, dying suddenly in a buggy accident. Her *mamm* said Ruth was in her early twenties when it happened. Ruth went ahead and moved into the house Daniel had built for their married life together. She was an attractive woman of medium height with light brown hair and a warm smile that lit up her whole face. Judith thought it sad that Ruth never found someone else she wanted to marry.

But maybe God meant for Ruth to be a teacher and that was why she never felt the desire to get married. Or maybe she'd never gotten over her first and only love so decided never to marry anyone. *Ruth doesn't seem to mind being single. She even mentioned how her scholars are her family and she seemed froh about it.* When they put the two classes together for reading, so that the older scholars could help the younger ones, it was fun for her and Ruth to teach together.

She sighed, wishing again she could have more education than an eighth grade one. Amish children only attended school for eight years, and their teachers only needed the same amount of schooling. A young college woman, Eliza Dunbar, had phoned their school and asked if she could visit. She wanted to observe for a college course and to interview Ruth. Although Ruth gave Miss Dunbar permission to visit, she didn't want to be interviewed. Ruth thought younger Judith would be more interesting for the interview.

Judith agreed to answer questions because she thought it'd be fun. But she also wanted to learn more about the young college student's life. What would it be like to continue your education by attending college? What an accomplishment it must be to graduate from college. If she hadn't been born Amish, going to college would be a realistic option for her. Actually going to high school would have been mandatory had she been born in a non-Amish family.

Wanting to get her GED was a reason she decided not to join the Amish church when her older sister Rachel did. She had planned on it because sharing her baptism event with her big sister seemed special. But she reconsidered because joining would close the door to any future learning. Once a person became baptized in the Amish church and accepted the rules of the *Ordnung*, higher education beyond eighth grade was forbidden. If she'd been baptized with Rachel and Katie, then sometime in the future decided to study and get her high school diploma, she would be shunned. She loved her family and scholars so any further education had to be before she joined the Amish church. She couldn't bear to be shunned.

She'd disappointed her *daed* but Rachel understood why she chose to wait longer to join. Rachel had waited until age twenty-one to be baptized, and was glad she first experienced a bit of the English world. *I admired Rachel for going to Florida last spring to learn more about English women's health and their stress in life.* Did non-Amish women live longer and better lives because they weren't Amish? Rachel wanted answers because *Mamm* died when only forty-four years old. After she died, Rachel wasn't sure about getting baptized and getting married to Samuel. Their *mamm* died from a heart attack, and they hadn't been able to call an ambulance with no phone shanty or access to the neighbors' phone the day of her mother's attack. Rachel blamed their *daed* for not putting a phone in somewhere on their property. Even though Bishop Amos didn't allow phones in their houses, they were allowed to have a phone in a barn or another outside building.

When Aunt Carrie had asked their *daed* if Rachel could visit and go on spring vacation with them, it'd been an answer to all of the Hershbergers' prayers. While away Rachel realized how life wasn't easy whether you were English or Amish. Each had stresses and burdens. Rachel worked through a lot of issues by prayer and listening to God's voice while enjoying the quiet morning time on the beach. When she returned to Fields Corner, Rachel was able to join the church and to move on with her life.

Judith finished eating her apple and threw the core away in the wastebasket. Glancing again at the children, she saw Jacob Weaver talking and laughing with her twin brothers, Noah and Matthew. *I wonder what he wants. He must be on his lunch break.* Jacob worked at the lumberyard in Fields Corner. He was a good son, helping his *daed* as much as possible with milking their cows and getting the crops out in the spring.

Jacob left the boys to talk to Ruth. After a moment, the older teacher pointed to the school. *Jacob must want to talk to me, but he never has anything much to say when our families get together.* Her *mamm* and Martha Weaver had been best friends for years. Both women hoped their children, Rachel and Samuel, would marry. When it happened in November, Rachel said, "*Mamm* would be so happy about my wedding."

A blast of cold air hit her when Jacob opened the outside door. She smiled at him as he removed his felt black hat and noticed his brown hair was darker than Samuel's. She liked how his longer hair curled. "What brings you here? Do you want to learn math?"

He laughed. "Math was my best subject but I could use help in writing."

"That's right. I remember you were good in math."

"I'm not surprised you're a teacher here." He took several steps toward her. "You were always one of the best scholars."

She remained seated as he stood by her desk. "*Danki*, Jacob."

"I talked to your brothers outside. They said they miss having you for a teacher."

"They behaved for me last year in fourth grade, but outside of school they both can be a handful."

Jacob laughed. "They are braver than I was at their age. I couldn't believe they tried to travel by themselves to Florida to see Rachel."

How well she remembered that time when Noah and Matthew missed Rachel the short time she was away. Rachel had taken over a lot of the duties of their mother. The twins especially missed her spending time with them each night before they went to sleep. Apparently Rachel had followed their mother's nightly routine of asking about their day. She listened as they shared what was good about their day as well as what wasn't so great. Rachel sometimes talked to them how much *Mamm* had loved them. Her brothers got it in their heads they should take a bus to see Rachel while she visited with their cousin Violet and Aunt Carrie. Fortunately, Bishop Amos saw them before they got a ride to the bus station. "They seem to thrive on adventures but Samuel's been a big help with them now."

"You have a full house with Samuel and Rachel living with you, but I think it's *gut* he decided to wait and build their house in the spring."

She watched Jacob start turning his hat and fingering the brim of his hat. *I don't think he came in here to talk about my brothers,* she realized. "The children's recess will be over soon. If you'd like to stay, I can have you speak to them about how important it is to listen to me." She gave a nervous giggle.

He blurted, "I'd like you to go sledding with me this Sunday. I never see you stay for the youth singing, so thought I'd ask you now."

Jacob caught her off guard, and she wasn't sure what to answer. At eighteen years of age, she had never been courted. It was partly her own fault because she hadn't attended the Sunday singings. Usually an Amish boy around the age of seventeen or older would ask a girl he was interested in if he could take her home after the Sunday singing. She pretty much devoted her time to her family and to teaching. Reading books and grading school papers took some of her time. But she also enjoyed being a scribe for the newspaper, *The Budget*. Writing the weekly letters about the news in Fields Corner to submit to the Amish newspaper was a precious pastime to her. *I want to get married and have a family someday, but not sure if I should go sledding with Jacob.* It wasn't because he was a few months younger, but because she never had gone with any young man to a youth get-together. "I don't know." Turning her head, she looked out the window and back at Jacob's face.

He grinned at her. "Were you checking to see if there's snow? You can't use that for an excuse. If you don't feel like sledding, we can do something else."

If she didn't go sledding with Jacob, she'd never hear the end of it from Rachel. She'd been pressuring her for months to get over her shyness and to stay for the Sunday youth gatherings. They were held every other church week for the young people. Rachel asked her frequently: "How will you find a life partner if you never socialize?"

He cleared this throat. "My lunch break is almost over. You can check your schedule. I'll stop by later this week to get your answer."

"I don't have any plans for Sunday and I'd like to go sledding. *Danki* for asking me." His gray eyes lit with pleasure at her answer. She hoped he'd still be happy he asked her after Sunday evening.

"*Gut.* I'll look forward to seeing you on Sunday. Be sure to wear your snow boots and wear a heavy coat. I don't want our fine Amish teacher getting sick."

"*Ya*, I will."

"Bye, Judith."

After she murmured bye to Jacob and he left the building, it occurred to her that she didn't know where the sledding was going to be. *Maybe Jacob plans on coming to my house so we can go in his buggy.* A flutter of excitement went through her at the aspect of riding in a buggy with Jacob. This was a first for her. He might be planning for her to stay for the Sunday afternoon gathering after church. This was their district's week to have Sunday church. No, he probably wouldn't pick her up but would take her home after sledding.

Before she could think too much about Jacob's surprise invitation, Judith turned when she heard female chatter in the hallway. Ruth's classroom was in the back of the schoolhouse with a door to the outside. An attractive young woman with strawberry blonde hair entered the classroom with Ruth. She wore black pants with a gray winter jacket. "Judith, this is the college student, Eliza Dunbar, I told you about. If we treat her right today, she might want to visit again."

Eliza Dunbar must have made quite an impression on Ruth. She definitely wanted the college student to be interested in a repeat observation of their Amish teaching methods. Judith extended her hand to Eliza and said, "Well, we better give you our warmest welcome then. I'm happy to meet you."

"I'm delighted to meet you too," Eliza said while shaking her hand. "I was just telling Ruth how much I appreciate this opportunity to observe both of you in the classroom."

"I showed her my room and thought it'd be nice for Eliza to observe you the first part of the afternoon and after our short recess she can observe my scholars. How does that sound?" Ruth asked.

Judith nodded. "That sounds *gut*."

"Lunch time and recess is almost over but I'll give you two a few minutes to talk before I have the children come inside. They are good children but I better get out there."

"Thank you again. I'm thrilled to be here," the young woman said to Ruth before turning back to Judith.

"I like your name. It reminds me of Eliza Doolittle from *My Fair Lady*."

"My mom played Eliza in a school production of My Fair Lady and decided then if she ever had a daughter she'd name her Eliza. Did you see a play of *My Fair Lady*?"

Judith shook her head. "I didn't see a play but I read George Bernard Shaw's play, *Pygmalion*."

"Your classroom is so cheery." Eliza glanced at the wall with the children's artwork of their favorite animals.

"Thank you. We are going to do arithmetic when the children come in from recess. There's a chair in the back of the room, but we can move it to the front." Judith pointed to a row of hooks on the wall by the door. "You can put your jacket on a hook."

"Sitting in the back is fine with me. I hope you don't mind if I take notes on my iPad. I like typing better than writing by hand." Eliza chuckled. "My handwriting sometimes is illegible. Not great for a future schoolteacher."

"That's no problem."

Eliza stared at the blackboard. "When I become a teacher, I wonder if the school I'm in will have blackboards or whiteboards."

Judith tucked a loose strand of blonde hair back under her *kapp*. "Sometimes I think a whiteboard would be nicer so we wouldn't have the chalk dust. Weaver's Bakery uses a whiteboard for their specials."

Eliza walked closer to a bulletin board they had recently decorated with snowflakes. "I love this with each snowflake labeled with the name of a pupil."

She was pleased that Eliza noticed the artwork the students did themselves. "The older children helped the younger ones. This exercise gave the primary graders experience in cutting and pasting and printing and reading their names. The older scholars enjoyed helping the younger ones." She pointed to a house in the wintry scene. A square was used for the house with a red triangle for the roof and small squares for the windows. A rectangle was pasted on for the chimney. "We reinforced the shape names for the young scholars with constructing the house."

"This is a great way to teach various shapes," Eliza said in an enthusiastic voice. "I enjoyed seeing several businesses in Fields Corner. It's bigger than I expected. I plan on stopping at the bakery after our interview. I want to buy the whoopie pies I've heard so much about."

"How about we go to Weaver's Bakery right after school? We can get coffee and dessert. My sister Rachel works at the bakery so you can meet her." *I want to have time to ask Eliza questions about college. Not only will Eliza learn about our Plain way of life, but I'll get a chance to learn more about higher education.*

* * *

As soon as Jacob returned to the lumberyard, his boss Mike asked, "How'd it go? Do you have a date?"

"Yep," Jacob answered.

"Give me five." Mike put his hand up in the air.

After slapping Mike's hand, Jacob moved away quickly to start loading a truck for a shipment that was going to Milford, about a fifty-minute drive from Fields Corner. Mike was a talkative guy, and he didn't want to be questioned about Judith. No need to tell his boss how Judith hesitated before saying yes to going sledding with him. It took him a long time to get courage to ask her. Now he wondered if he'd made a mistake. *Did she think I'm not bright enough for her? She's a scribe for the The Budget. Samuel said she hadn't been courted so I thought she might be a little eager to go sledding with me. Maybe Judith doesn't like sledding. No, that's not it. She wasn't sure about going with me.* Although his confidence took a hit from her hesitation in saying yes, it couldn't be all him. Judith wasn't the first girl he'd asked out for the Sunday get-togethers. A year ago he'd courted Leah Hostetler a few times, but she'd moved away before they could get serious about each other.

"Hey, Jacob," Mike yelled. "Have you ever thought of getting your driver's license? It'd be a big help for me if you could drive some of the shipments."

"Don't you remember I'm Amish? I don't think driving one of your big trucks would be the same as my buggy." Mike appeared by his side so he stopped loading and wiped his sweaty forehead with his sleeve. *You can't miss Mike when he stands by you,* Jacob thought. *He's a huge guy, even his neck is thick.* But Mike blamed his large neck on wrestling. He'd wrestled while in high school and college in the heavyweight class.

"You said during you *rumspringa* you could get your license. I didn't know that you had joined your church."

"I haven't joined." Leaning against the wagon of the truck, Jacob continued, "A few of my friends have gone together and bought a car so that's why I mentioned getting my license. I'm not sure what my parents would do. They might ask me to move out." He didn't think his parents would tell him to leave home and might look the other way, but he wasn't so sure about Judith's *daed*. He'd been interested in Judith Hershberger for a long time. Baptized or not, he wanted to see what happened when he took Judith sledding. He hoped she'd want to see him again and if she did, he didn't want to upset her *daed* by doing something English like driving a truck.

"I don't want to cause any problems for you with your folks but if you decide to get your license, let me know."

Jacob grinned at Mike. "You'll be the first to know. If I drive one of your trucks, you better have good insurance."

Mike laughed. "No problem on the insurance."

After the truck was filled with the lumber order, Jacob opened a Coke to drink. He needed the caffeine before cutting trestles. He hadn't slept much last night, thinking about seeing Judith. He didn't remember feeling this *naerfich* when he'd first asked Leah out. Maybe it was because Leah had attended the youth gatherings, so he'd talked to her a few times first before asking her for a date.

He fingered the cold Coke can while he couldn't stop thinking about Judith. Sure, he knew her from their families being close, but she'd always been quiet when the Weavers and Hershbergers used to get together. Many times she'd go off with Katie when Samuel and Rachel were busy talking. And they hadn't gotten together as much since Irene Hershberger passed on. Irene had been his *mamm's* best friend. Now that Samuel and Rachel had married in November, they enjoyed visiting with Rachel's brother, Peter and his wife, Ella.

Judith looked pretty in her blue dress with her bright blue eyes in a delicate face. She was the prettiest teacher Fields Corner Amish School ever had...probably not only the prettiest, but the smartest one too. Samuel told him that Judith had changed her mind about joining the church with Katie and Rachel because she wanted to study and get her her high school diploma. Why would she want to do that when she was Amish? She didn't need more education to teach in their Amish school. Was she thinking about going elsewhere to teach? He hoped not. *One thing for sure, I better think of interesting things to discuss with Judith on Sunday. I enjoy reading her letters in The Budget. That will be a good topic for us. I can also ask her about her scholars. She likes to read, but I haven't read any books lately so that's out.*

With both of them not being baptized, he hoped Mr. Hershberger wouldn't object if they started dating. They shouldn't officially date until both were baptized, but Rachel wasn't baptized when she dated Samuel. And they were just going sledding as friends, not as boyfriend and girlfriend. *I'm getting way ahead of myself here. I just need to get through Sunday evening. I hope that Judith will want to spend more time with me, even though I don't like to read. Hey, they say opposites attract.*

Chapter Two

"I'm glad you suggested doing the interview here at the bakery." Eliza sipped her coffee. She glanced toward the window by their table. "It's such a dreary day but it's cozy being in here."

Delicious smells wafted through the bakery. "I love teaching but was ready to escape the schoolroom." Judith tucked a loose tendril of blonde hair into her *kapp*.

"The whoopie pies are delicious. I'm going to buy more to take home." After Eliza swallowed a bite of whoopie pie, she used her napkin to wipe chocolate off her lips. "I guess we better get started. Ruth mentioned that you're around my age. I'm impressed you're already a teacher. In my world we have to go at least four years and get a degree. I'm only in my second year and will have to do student teaching while in college. Did you have to do any student teaching before becoming a teacher?"

Judith nodded. "After I graduated from eighth grade, I observed Ruth teaching the upper grades and at this time, Miss Miller taught the lower grades. The Amish school board recommend that if you want to teach, you should be an apprentice first. I observed for a year and was a teacher's aide. After I did this, I did what you call student teaching because I taught in Ruth's classroom and also did in the lower grades. I was nervous but I was happy to have this experience. Both teachers were helpful and made suggestions while I first taught the scholars."

Eliza typed on her iPad for a moment, then looked up at Judith. "That's something I noticed earlier. You and Ruth call your students scholars. Is that common in Amish schools?"

"*Ya*, it is."

"Did you take any correspondence courses or have any kind of help that wasn't from the Amish teachers here?"

"*Ya*, I did take correspondence courses...that made my parents happy to see me keeping the Amish philosophy of staying apart from the world."

"Well, you're an excellent teacher from what I observed today so you saved a ton of money and time by not having to get a degree to teach."

Judith exhaled a deep breath. "Even though additional schooling isn't necessary in the Amish community to become a teacher, I'd love to experience more learning myself. I wanted to have my GED by now but I haven't had time to study. My sister Rachel got married in November so we were busy getting ready for it."

"I can help you study for it. It'll be fun." Eliza sipped her coffee. "You should talk to Ruth about it."

"I'm not sure Ruth would be encouraging." Judith shrugged. "She never expressed any interest in getting her GED. And our school board members look for the person to have a deep religious faith, interest in teaching, and an ability to handle children. They don't expect their teachers to have more than an eighth grade education."

"I'll get the information for you anyhow, so you can look it over. I'll be happy to help you in any way I can. Getting your GED is a wonderful goal for you."

"*Danki*, Eliza. I appreciate it." *Such a gut day...first Jacob asked me to go sledding with him on Sunday and now Eliza wants to help me get my GED.*

"You're very welcome." Eliza patted her arm. "How old were you when you took the teaching position to teach the first four grades?"

"I was seventeen. When Miss Miller got married, she quit teaching so I took her position and started teaching the lower grades."

"I'm sure teaching the younger students helped because of your age. Teaching an eighth grade would be difficult when you aren't that much older than the students. It seems like discipline would be a problem when you're so young."

Judith shrugged. "It's not. It's common for Amish teachers not to be much older than the scholars. Ruth was younger than I was when she had all the classes. She's been teaching since she was fifteen. When she started here, the school had fewer children. Fields Corner keeps growing."

"I imagine that growth helps to fund the school."

"It helps for us to be productive and earn money for many things. Amish schools don't receive any tax money so all the expenses are paid by the school families. We pay taxes but don't take any money from the government."

Eliza's eyebrows shot up. "I've never visited an Amish community and you're the first Amish person I've talked to. It's hard for me to comprehend not receiving any tax money for your school. Even our parochial schools receive government money for special services for remedial math and speech plus ride the public school buses."

"Our children walk to school no more than a mile or two, or in bad weather are driven by buggy. I walk to school sometimes with my brothers, Matthew and Noah. In the warmer months, they might ride their scooters and the older children are allowed to have bikes but not fancy ones." Jabbing a fork in her pie, she continued, "We don't have any expenses like a non-Amish school. I'm sure you noticed that we don't have expensive computers, televisions, or other electronic equipment. Our children bring their lunches so that eliminates the need for kitchen and cafeteria facilities. We don't have to buy expensive physical equipment either. When you came today, you might have seen the children were playing a high-energy running game of tag. And the older students played softball. This was the first day they were outside this month. They've been playing board games and ping pong in the basement because of the cold weather."

"I loved jumping rope during recess when I was in elementary school." Eliza's smiled. "Actually I jump rope now for exercise but it's not as much fun jumping by myself. Do the children like to jump rope?"

"The younger ones do." Judith grinned at Eliza. "You can visit again and jump rope with them."

"I'm surprised Judith doesn't jump with them. Or do you?" Rachel asked as she stood by their table.

Judith shook her head at Rachel's teasing and noticed the glow on her face. Her sister was beautiful before her marriage to Samuel, but now she seemed even more so. Married life definitely agreed with Rachel. "I haven't. Eliza, this is my sister, Rachel Weaver."

Rachel extended her hand to Eliza and said, "Hello, Eliza. It's nice to meet you."

Eliza shook Rachel's hand. "I'm happy to meet you too."

"Are you done for the day?" *I hope Rachel is because I'd like to stay longer and ask Eliza questions about being able to go to college to further one's education. Even though I can't go to college, I want to know what it's like.*

"*Ya*, I'm just waiting on the twins." Rachel smoothed her white apron. "I thought I'd take them home, so you two can have more time for your interview. Besides, it's gotten windy and colder so I hate for them to walk home."

"They have classroom duty this week but should be finished soon." Judith turned away from Rachel to look at Eliza. "That's another thing. We don't have to pay a janitor. The children take turns helping to clean the classrooms. Of course, Ruth and I clean our rooms too, but it's nice to teach the children to have responsibility for their schoolroom."

"And the fathers help with the school maintenance. I hope you don't mind if I sit here while I wait for the boys." Rachel didn't wait for an answer and pulled a chair from under the table.

Judith thought, *I'd like to tell Rachel about Jacob but don't want to in front of Eliza. She might ask about Amish dating. I don't feel like talking about something that I have never personally experienced.*

"Did you make the whoopie pies, Rachel?" Eliza asked. "They are so yummy. It's a good thing I don't work in Fields Corner, I'd be eating here all the time and probably gain weight."

Eliza was thin and pretty in her black pants and lavender sweater. Judith couldn't imagine her putting on weight. "I doubt that would happen. You'd probably get tired of Amish food. Even though Rachel's a fantastic cook, we enjoy getting pizza or something different sometimes."

Rachel nodded. "I liked eating at Applebee's and other restaurants when we went to the beach."

"I love the colors of your dresses. I thought Amish women wore only dark colors like black and gray," Eliza stared at them. "But you both are so pretty in your blue and green dresses. And I noticed the boys wore blue shirts instead of white with black pants."

"*Ya*, we're allowed to wear certain colors such as blue, lavender, and green. Our community decides the set of colors that are allowed. The most common shades are taken from nature." Judith watched Eliza typing her answer on her iPad. *I wonder if all the college students use iPads.*

Rachel added, "Each district is different so some might be more limited in their color choices. I know some Amish women in their communities are allowed only to wear black or blue dresses. After a member dies, the immediate family wears black for a year of mourning."

"That's interesting," Eliza said. "Oh, I noticed Ruth's prayer covering on her head was black and you both wear white. Is there a certain age when you switch to black?"

"You're very observant. It used to be that any single girl or woman wore a black *kapp* or prayer covering. You switch to white when you marry. But a couple of years ago our bishop gave us permission to wear white during the week if we prefer. It's actually easier to clean the white ones than the black *kapps*. But when we attend church service, single girls must wear black *kapps*," Judith explained.

Eliza chuckled slightly. "I guess that way the men know which women are available."

When the door opened with a chime, Rachel looked pleased at seeing the twins enter the bakery. "*Gut*, the boys are here. I want to get home and get supper started."

Eliza smiled at Matthew and Noah. "I enjoyed being in your class. You both did great doing your fractions."

"*Danki* for checking our answers," Matthew said. "Are you coming home with us, Miss Dunbar? I want to show you our new pony."

Eliza must have made an impression on my brothers, Judith thought. "She can't right now. She's interviewing me for her college class."

Rachel stood next to the twins and asked Eliza, "Why don't you join us for supper after you finish here? Judith can ride with you since I'm taking the buggy."

"I would like to visit your home but I don't want to impose." Eliza glanced at Rachel first, then Judith. "Are you sure it'll be okay with your mother?"

"*Mamm* died from a heart attack.," Noah answered quickly. "That's why Samuel moved in our house after he married Rachel so she could stay with us."

Matthew nodded. "I'm glad Rachel didn't move. It's great having both sisters live with us."

"I'm so sorry about your mother." Eliza's blue eyes looked moist and she paused for a moment. "My dad passed away from cancer recently. It's been hard on us so I understand how painful it is to lose a parent."

"I'm sorry you lost your father. You've been through a lot too," Judith said.

Rachel murmured condolences, then put her coat on. "Let's go boys." Turning to Eliza, she said, "It was nice meeting you. Whatever you decide about supper will be fine. Judith planned on getting a ride home with Samuel so if you can't make it, we won't make her walk home."

"I'd love to come. Thank you so much for inviting me." Eliza grinned. "I guess the more I learn about your wonderful Amish life, the better it'll be for me. This interview is actually for my sociology class, but observing the classes today was also for an education class."

Rachel smiled back at Eliza. "Oh, I see. You're killing two birds with one stone. You better soak up as much information as you can."

"We don't want to be responsible for you getting a low grade in either course so you should visit and eat supper with us." *I might get a chance to ask Eliza what it's like going to high school and college,* Judith thought.

Noah's green eyes widened. "You can help us name our pony."

* * *

Rachel opened the oven door. "Meatloaf should be done. I'll turn off the oven. The boys sure took to Eliza. I wonder if she can help them name their pony."

"*Danki* for inviting Eliza to supper," Judith said, as she set the table with their white china. She'd decided to use her mother's good dishes. "She offered to help me study for my GED."

"I'm glad you're making plans to get your GED, but maybe you shouldn't talk about it in front of *Daed*. He's afraid if you receive more education, you won't join our church." Rachel gave Judith a worried look. "Is that why you're making plans with Eliza so you can live in the English world?"

"I loved my childhood but Amish girls learn how to be good wives and mothers. We're taught how to cook, bake, quilt, clean, raise children, and drive buggies." She grinned at Rachel. "Well, I guess I never learned the cooking and baking part."

Rachel put slabs of butter in the pan with the hot potatoes. "You have made *wunderbaar* progress in the kitchen. Besides you love to sew and quilt. And your quilts have earned money for the family and for the school."

"I don't plan on leaving our community and our way of life, and I want to get married someday but..." her voice trailed off because she wasn't sure how much to share with her sister.

"But what?"

"I want something different right now. I'd like to learn more than we are allowed in our Amish schools." Judith sighed. "Some days I don't know what I want, but I do yearn for more education."

"Maybe you can take a course in bookkeeping." Rachel stopped mashing the potatoes and looked at Judith. "I went to the fabric store during a break, and Sarah told me how she doesn't have time to do what she enjoys in the store. She's always stuck with the business part and she hates doing financial stuff."

"You're so clever." Judith laughed. "You know Bishop Amos would approve of me learning accounting. I remember Martha Weaver took an accounting class before she started her bakery."

Samuel walked into the room, removing his felt hat and putting it on one of the pegs by the kitchen door. "Rachel is clever. She married me."

Rachel chuckled. "Your siblings might not agree with me being clever marrying you."

Samuel kissed Rachel on the cheek, then he glanced at Judith. "Talking about siblings, I'm glad you accepted Jacob's invitation to go sledding. He was *naerfich* about asking you and afraid you might turn him down. He's liked you for a long time."

"What?" Rachel gave Judith a surprised look. "When did this happen? I can't believe you never mentioned it."

"I meant to tell you at the bakery but didn't want to in front of Eliza. It's embarrassing this is my first date at my age. Jacob came to see me at school and asked me while the children were outside playing."

"I'm going to wash up. I'm hungry. I'll leave you two to talk about my *bruder's* visit."

"I'm glad you accepted. I saw Jacob watching you with interest, and Samuel mentioned he liked you. This is an excellent time for you two to have fun together. Jacob hasn't been baptized so you are both on the same path in trying to decide whether to join the church or not. Or *when* to join, hopefully." Rachel squeezed her shoulder. "I'm glad I waited until I was twenty-one to get baptized. It's best you wait and are sure before joining."

Judith smoothed her white apron and thought, *God created me with a strong desire to keep learning. Does He want me to learn more by becoming part of the English world? Or to become a good Amish wife and mother and to forget about getting my GED? I never expected anyone to ask me out. Now that it happened, I am feeling doubts. It's been my fault for being too shy to attend the Sunday sings. Can I have both dreams...to be an Amish wife and mother and to continue to receive more education? Rachel didn't join until she was twenty-one so I have time but if I use this time to get my GED, what if I want more education? Bishop Amos will question why I want more if I'm going to join the Amish church. Getting more education might prevent me from teaching in the Fields Corner Amish School. I love my scholars.*

Judith prayed silently, *Lord, help me on my journey in life to make the right decisions. What I yearn for might not be what You want me to do. I don't want to lose what I already have in my life...a wunderbaar family and my teaching career by pushing toward more education. If it's right for me to study for my GED, please give me the assurance that it's the right thing to do.*

Chapter Three

Eliza took a bite of meatloaf and couldn't believe she was sitting at a table with an Amish family. *I know so little about their faith. I don't want to offend them or hurt their feelings.* Her tendency to blurt out things had gotten her in trouble in the past. Her last boyfriend informed her that she needed to be more conscious of what she said to people. And what could she talk about here at the table? She obviously couldn't mention recent movies or television shows she watched. Or books she read because maybe they were only allowed to read certain ones.

As she glanced around at each person at the huge table, Eliza saw so much kindness in their faces. These people weren't that different from her own family. Sure, their dress was totally different from her world with the guys wearing black pants with suspenders and the women wearing long dresses with aprons. *It's interesting how Rachel and Judith keep their white coverings on their heads at all times,* she thought. But she could tell that they cared about the same things her family did and wanted the best for each other.

Even the kitchen appeared a bit like hers. They might not have electricity but their kitchen had a refrigerator and not an icebox like she expected. Not all Amish must follow the same guidelines in their faith, Eliza realized. On the drive to their house, Judith had mentioned something about using gas in the bakery instead of electricity. Gas-powered refrigerators and stoves must also be allowed in their homes.

Glancing around the kitchen, she noticed the mostly plain white walls with light oak cabinets. Uncluttered countertops caught her attention where at her home they had many electrical appliances. She noticed a mixer with a crank. *Wow, that must be difficult with all the baking Rachel and Judith did daily to have to rely on turning the crank to mix the ingredients.* "Rachel, the meatloaf is delicious and I love the sauce on top. I'd like the recipe."

"*Danki*, Eliza. The sauce has ketchup, brown sugar, water, garlic powder and liquid smoke but I'll give you the recipe before you leave."

"I never heard of liquid smoke."

Rachel took a sip of milk. "I don't use it often but like to in my meatloaf because it adds a smoky flavor to the meat."

"Eliza came up with two names for our pony," Noah said. "Minnie because she's so small or Pinto because she's spotted."

"She's small but very strong," Matthew said. "I like both names. I can't wait to train her."

Judith looked at Eliza and said, "Matthew loves training ponies and he recently trained a pony for a family with three little girls."

"I'm impressed. That's quite an accomplishment." Eliza scooped up mashed potatoes with her fork. "I had a pony when I was little. Her name was Powerpuff."

"What happened to your pony?" Noah asked.

"When we moved to Cincinnati, we didn't have a barn for her, so we sold Powerpuff to a neighbor." Eliza tucked a lock of hair behind her ear.

"Did you ride her with a saddle or have her pull a wagon?" Matthew asked.

"I rode her with a saddle. My friends loved visiting so they could take rides on Powerpuff."

Noah put another piece of meatloaf on his plate. "What about your mother? Does she like horses and ponies?"

Eliza nodded. "Yes, I think so." *Why does Noah want to know if my mom likes horses? Where did that come from?*

Noah and Matthew exchanged pleased looks.

Matthew asked, "Do you think your mother would like to go on a buggy ride?"

Eliza laughed. "I suppose so. But hey, how about giving me a buggy ride first?"

Noah's green eyes widened. "We like you a lot, Eliza, and thought your mom must be nice, too, so maybe she could marry our *daed*."

Matthew gave an eager nod. "*Daed* doesn't want to be stuck with Bishop Amos' sister. We don't care for her either. She told us we needed a switch taken to our behinds."

The boys' father choked on something, then he cleared his throat. "Boys, that's enough. Sometimes I think you both need a spanking."

So that was why the twins had asked her so many questions in the barn about her mother. She had thought it was because they missed theirs and wanted to learn more about her non-Amish mom. Should she point out the obvious reason her mom couldn't marry their father? Eliza wondered.

"I'm sure Mrs. Dunbar is a lovely lady but she wouldn't want to marry *Daed*," Judith pointed out. "It'd be hard for her to change from being English to Amish."

"Besides, she doesn't even know *Daed*." Rachel tucked a loose strand of blonde hair back under her *kapp*.

Eliza still couldn't believe the twins would want her mother to marry their dad. *Judith said they were ten years old so I'm surprised they'd even be thinking their father should remarry.* Also the boys had just met her so another reason why it seemed weird for them to mention her mother as a marriage prospect. But in a way, she could relate; she felt a bond with them quickly, too, which hadn't been hard. Matthew with his blond hair and blue eyes was adorable while Noah was also cute but in a different way. She noticed how sensitive he was and his brilliant green eyes didn't seem to miss a thing. "Even though my mother would love to meet all of you and ride in a buggy, her faith is as important to her as your Amish faith is to you." She smiled at Matthew and Noah.

"But you said she doesn't like computers and she likes to read from regular books," Noah said while he pulled on one of his suspenders. "And she doesn't like to drive her car and has you or your brother drive her places a lot."

"Noah, I'm not looking for a wife," Mr. Hershberger said in a firm voice. "No one can take your dear *mamm's* place."

Matthew gave a worried glance at his brother before looking at his father. "We just want you to be *froh, Daed*. And Mrs. Dunbar likes to cook and bake."

Samuel grinned at Rachel. "It sounds like your *bruders* want to replace you in the kitchen. I don't know why when you're an excellent cook."

"We heard you talking about building your house this spring. Rachel won't be here to cook for us when you move." Matthew hesitated for a moment, then continued, "Judith's getting better at cooking, but she'd rather read than make cookies."

Judith laughed. "I think you two could live on Rachel's cookies alone."

Mr. Hershberger stared at Noah and Matthew. "Remember Jesus said: 'Man shall not live on bread alone, but on every word that comes from the mouth of God.'"

"*Daed's* right. We can't live on food alone and need to listen to God's voice," Rachel said. After a moment, she turned to Eliza. "Well, talking about baking, how about a piece of pie, Eliza? I have butterscotch and apple."

"Both sound delicious but I've never had butterscotch pie so I'd love a piece of it."

"Everything Rachel makes is *gut* but I especially love her butterscotch pie," Samuel said.

"It's *gut* we like butterscotch pie because Rachel makes it *a lot*," Noah said.

Judith raised her eyebrows. "She spoils you two with all the time she spends baking your favorite cookies."

"Matthew and Noah, pick up the dishes and put them by the sink," Mr. Hershberger said.

While Rachel cut the pies, Judith poured coffee for the adults.

"Would you like to play checkers, Eliza, after you finish eating your pie?" Noah asked.

"That sounds like fun but first I want to do the dishes. Rachel's worked hard preparing supper and Judith's taught school all day." Eliza hoped she'd get a chance to learn a bit more about the Amish faith while she helped in the kitchen. She had many questions but didn't want to impose and make a nuisance of herself. Judith and Rachel had already been generous with their time.

Ten minutes later it was just Eliza and Judith standing next to a sink full of hot water and dishes. Judith laughed. "Everyone disappeared quickly. *Danki* for drying the dishes."

Eliza held a towel in her hand as she waited for the next clean dish. "I have a confession to make. I was sincere in my offer to help with the dishes, but I also want to ask more questions. I hope you don't mind."

Judith shook her head. "Of course not."

"I thought that Amish use wood stoves for cooking but noticed you have a gas stove."

"We've never had a wood stove for cooking. We've always had a gas stove as well as a gas refrigerator. Some

Amish districts are more conservative and are much more restrictive in what they allow in their lives. They use wood stoves. Also they don't have in-door plumbing like we do and still use outhouses. Riding in cars is prohibited, except for emergencies, in the more restrictive districts. But in our Amish district we are allowed to ride in cars." Judith stopped rinsing a plate to look at Eliza. "It's helpful because our *Aenti* Carrie invited us to Outer Banks last summer and we rode in their van. We never could've gone that far in a buggy."

"I never pictured Amish going to the beach. I'm glad you and your family got to go. I love the ocean. When my dad was alive, we used to go to the beach every summer."

"It was the first time for us to go to the beach except for Rachel. She went to Cocoa Beach with our *aenti* over spring break before she married Samuel."

"Well, even though you ride in cars at times, you still drive buggies most places. That must be hard to spend so much time getting places." *I don't want to hurt Judith's feelings,* Eliza thought, *but it seems like they are being hypocrites by saying they don't believe in owning cars...yet they'll ride in them when they wish.*

Judith slowly rinsed another plate. "It's calming to ride in a buggy except if people are in cars behind us and anxious to zoom around us. We strive to avoid worldliness and want to keep our families close to home. We don't want to have the convenience of being able to jump in a car and travel to faraway places in the world. Owning a car would cause too much mobility, and it'd cause a negative effect on our family life. We do hire English drivers when we need to travel longer distances and it'd take too long by buggy. Like to the hospital or for medical appointments or to visit relatives far away."

Eliza grinned. "If I help you to study for your GED test, maybe you can give me a buggy ride sometime."

"Definitely. You'll enjoy the slower pace and seeing more of the scenery."

"There's not too much to see now with the cold weather," Rachel said as she entered the kitchen, "but you should come back and take a buggy ride. We're working on a jigsaw puzzle. I thought I'd check to see if you need some help so you can join us."

"*Danki*, Rachel," Judith said, "but we'll almost done here."

Eliza turned around to look at Rachel. "I should be leaving soon but thank you so much for supper. Everything tasted so good. And I enjoyed visiting with all of you." *I almost hate to leave but it's a long drive home and I have a morning class tomorrow. What a fascinating family they are,* Eliza thought.

"Come back anytime to see us. You made a hit with Matthew and Noah." Rachel grinned. "Even your mother did and she wasn't even here."

Eliza laughed. "They are cute. I wish now I had a younger brother."

"Are you an only child?" Rachel asked.

Eliza shook her head. "I have a wonderful older brother, Austin. He's a sports writer for a newspaper in Columbus but fortunately, he comes home often to visit."

"Judith, did you tell Eliza you write the news for our area for *The Budget*?"

"No. I didn't even think to." Judith slid the meatloaf pan in the water and looked at Eliza. "I think you'd enjoy reading the letters and articles in *The Budget*. It'll give you more insight into our Amish life."

"I'd love to read them, especially what you've written." Eliza frowned. "I can't believe I forgot what Ruth told me. She said to ask you for copies to take home to read."

"I'll get you several except not the one *Daed's* reading now." Rachel giggled. "I don't see him being generous with his reading material. He's been absorbed in reading every word. He's probably trying to forget how people keep suggesting women for him to marry."

After Rachel left the kitchen, Eliza said, "Rachel's sweet. Everyone in your family is nice."

"When you mentioned your older brother, I realized that I didn't tell you we have an older brother Peter. He's married to Ella. Peter and Samuel have been *gut* and close friends for years."

Judith hadn't mentioned being serious about anyone. I don't want to be rude and pry into her personal life though. Ruth's also single so I wonder if Amish teachers are allowed to teach after they get married. "Are Amish teachers usually single? Or can they still teach after they get married?"

Judith handed her the pan to dry. "Usually when an Amish woman marries, she quits her job so that's why our female teachers are single. Sometimes there are a few exceptions and there might be a married teacher, but once children arrive they always quit teaching. Women might return to working outside the home when their youngest starts school. Rachel works part-time at the bakery and helps a friend with her catering business. But I think that's mainly so she can have lunch with Samuel a couple times a week."

I hope I can remember everything I've learned about the Amish, so I can write it down when I get home. "I know you have to get up early in the morning for school and I have to get up early, too, so I better be going."

"I'm glad you came today."

Removing her winter jacket from the peg on the wall, Eliza realized they hadn't made plans to get together to study for Judith's test. She didn't think they were allowed to have phones but she remembered Judith pointed to a small building on their property. She'd called it a phone shanty. "Maybe we can get together soon to study for your GED. Is it okay for me to call your family phone or should I call you at school?"

"I don't think Ruth would mind you calling me on the school phone, but I'll give you the number of our phone because I think that'll be easier. You can leave a message on the answering machine. We check daily for messages. It's so nice to finally have a phone for emergencies and to talk occasionally to friends and relatives. We aren't allowed to have phones in the house, but are allowed to have a phone in the barn or in a shanty."

Eliza pulled a post-it note off a pad and wrote her number down. "Here's my cell phone number so you have it."

"It must be great going to college." Judith sighed. "Maybe sometime you can tell me what it's like to be in college. I wish I could experience college life just for a day."

* * *

After telling everyone good-bye and leaving the Hershberger home, Eliza got into her Toyota Corolla. She put her key into the ignition, thinking how surprised she'd been when Judith had mentioned college. *I don't think getting her GED might be enough for Judith. It sounds like she's thinking what it'd be like to go to college.* From what she'd learned today, the Plain people thought an eighth grade education was sufficient in their Amish world. If Judith should decide to go to college after she gets her GED, her Amish family might reject her for wanting even more education. Or maybe not reject her but certainly they might not approve. Would Judith disregard their beliefs and do what she wanted?

She shivered in the cold car but knew in a few minutes it'd be warm. *I can't imagine being in a buggy on a cold winter night.* It could be romantic to ride in a buggy with the right guy. She wished she had someone special in her life but maybe it was just as well. She had a heavy course load this semester plus a part-time job at the hospital. She hadn't planned on staying so long today in Fields Corner but glad she did. She learned more about the Amish by being in the Hershberger home.

She'd been surprised that they all prayed silently before eating instead of out loud. At her household, they prayed together out loud. She'd been relieved that they enjoyed teasing each other while eating and were not stern like she'd expected. Rachel looked so young...well, at age twenty-one, she was. She got the impression that the Amish married in their early twenties. *I wonder if that's another reason Judith is anxious to get her GED because she knows marrying young is expected of her.* While she was in the barn admiring their new pony, Matthew and Noah mentioned Jacob had stopped to see Judith at school. Samuel said his brother asked Judith to go sledding.

David Hershberger then said to Samuel in a teasing tone, "Another Weaver man interested in one of my *dochdern*. What am I going to do?"

Although Ruth Yoder was single, she was probably in her thirties. She could easily still get married. She smiled, wondering if the twins had tried to match Ruth with their dad. Or did they think she was too young for him? A chuckle escaped her thinking how Matthew and Noah had suggested her mother could marry their dad. She couldn't wait to tell her mom there was an available Amish guy for her.

As she took the ramp to get on interstate, an idea hit her. Wouldn't it be something for her and Judith to switch places? She noticed how the non-Amish stared at Judith when they walked to the bakery. How would she handle dressing in a long dress and wearing an apron? Her hair couldn't show and she'd have to wear the prayer thing on her head.

I wonder if it would be disrespectful to them and to their faith to ask if I could dress like them for a couple of days. It'd help me to write a more revealing paper for my sociology class. Can I live without my smartphone and my iPad for a couple of days? I'd have to give up tweeting. It might be nice and peaceful to stay away from all electronic devices. Hey, I could learn to drive a buggy. Would Judith want to learn to drive a car?

Oh, I wish I could call Judith now and ask her if she'd want to experience some things for her rumspringa. She knew that they were allowed to do English...I love how they call us English...things during their running around time. I can buy her a cheap cell phone so it'll be easier to call each other. She could wear my clothes and go to my college classes.

A flash of sadness hit her at picturing Judith in her world. What if Judith changed drastically from experiencing college? I like her just the way she is.

Chapter Four

Before going to her bedroom where Samuel waited for her, Rachel entered the boys' room. She saw Matthew was reading a book and Noah was sketching. She watched them for a moment, thankful that after their wedding in November, they did what many newly married Amish couples did at first and lived with her family. When she'd gone to Cocoa Beach last spring with her *Aenti* Carrie, Samuel wrote her that the house building could wait, so that her brothers would still have her with them if she decided to marry him. Even though the land he'd bought was only fifteen minutes away by buggy, she would be able to do something that was crucial to her and to Matthew and Noah—she could tuck them in at night and listen to how their day had gone for them. She started this after their *mamm* had passed away. She wasn't trying to replace her mother, but knew the nightly routine had been important to Matthew and Noah. It had become so important to them that the brothers made plans to leave home by themselves to visit her in Florida.

Fortunately, Bishop Amos had stopped them from leaving Fields Corner and drove them back home.

She smiled at them. "You two seemed to enjoy Eliza's visit."

Noah leaned to the edge of the bed and put his colored pencils and art pad on the nightstand. "I like Eliza. She's a lot of fun."

Matthew smiled. "Today was a *gut* day...we met Eliza. Too bad she couldn't stay to work on the puzzle."

"I wish *Mamm* could have met Eliza," Noah said. "She would've loved her. *Mamm* loved Sharon Maddox and visiting with her."

Matthew nodded. "She said it was nice to have a friend like Sharon living close by."

"I hope we'll see Eliza again. For a girl, she's all right." Noah grinned at Rachel.

"I like her too. So did you choose a name for your pony?" Rachel didn't voice her concerns that maybe Eliza might have too much influence over Judith. She got the feeling that Judith was interested in knowing more about college classes and that worried her a little. She hoped that Judith wouldn't want to continue her education after she passed her GED test.

"We decided on Minnie." Matthew pointed to his brother's art pad. "Show Rachel the picture you drew of Minnie."

Noah picked up his art pad and flipped it open to a picture of their pony.

Rachel turned the pad so she could see it better. "Noah, this is a beautiful drawing. It looks just like Minnie."

Matthew murmured to Noah, "I think you should show Rachel the other picture you drew."

Noah exhaled a deep breath and flipped the page to a drawing of a woman. "I was afraid I'd forget what *Mamm* looked like so I drew this of her. Do you think it looks like her?"

Rachel was quiet as she stared closely at the woman's face, recognizing their sweet *mamm*. Her eyes filled with tears and she felt sad that Noah had to draw a picture of his mother so he could always remember what she looked like. *Should I show them the hidden picture I have of Mamm?* she wondered. Aunt Carrie had given her a picture of her mother last spring before they left Florida. Since Amish weren't allowed to take pictures of each other, she hadn't said anything to the boys. She was afraid they'd tell others, and she'd get in trouble with Bishop Amos before she even joined the church. She hadn't even told Samuel she had a picture. But she always planned on giving them a picture of their mother to keep when they were a little older. *Aenti* Carrie gave one to Judith too.

Drawing people was another forbidden part of the whole picture rule. Nature scenes and animals were fine to draw. Even people could be drawn as long as their faces didn't show. Her cousin Violet had a hard time understanding this rule in their *Ordnung* but it was because having a picture of oneself was an unacceptable act of pride. Bishop Amos mentioned frequently the second commandment about "making graven images" and he referred to a rendering of a face as a graven image.

I'm not going to mention that Noah shouldn't have drawn a picture of Mamm. She's not here so pride is not involved in this instance. I'll ask Aunt Carrie to give each boy a picture on her next visit. "It's a beautiful drawing, Noah, and it looks just like her. I love it and *danki* for showing it to me."

As Rachel tucked her brothers in, she said, "*Gut nacht*. Say your prayers and I'll see you in the morning." On her way out, she turned off the small low power bedside lamp that gave off enough light for reading. She remembered how surprised Eliza was to see they had some battery power lights and gas lights instead of candles or all kerosene lanterns. Their *daed* did like to have a few kerosene lamps so they were in their living room.

In the hallway she saw Judith's bedroom door open so looked in and noticed her sister was reading at her desk. "Sweet dreams tonight. Maybe you'll dream about Jacob."

Judith turned away from her book to smile. "Or I might dream about Eliza helping me to study for my GED. *Danki* so much for inviting her to supper tonight. And for taking the boys home with you so I could answer more of her questions."

"I'm glad God brought Eliza into your life. I know you could easily get your GED without her help, but it'll be nice for you to have a study partner." Rachel shrugged. "But I think it works two ways. It's good for Eliza to learn more about our Amish community. There seems to be wrong information about us and our beliefs. I'm sure she'll do a good job writing the truth."

Judith's blue eyes widened. "I'm a bit *naerfich* about going sledding with Jacob."

Finally, Jacob enters the conversation, Rachel thought. "You've known Jacob for a long time so that'll make it easier. You two will have a *gut* time together. And you loved sledding when you were younger."

"Okay, big *schweschder.* Your words of wisdom helped. I'm glad Jacob asked me. I should be able to survive Sunday evening."

Rachel leaned against the doorframe. "I'm glad. I better scoot to bed. *Gut nacht.*"

As she left Judith's room, she saw Samuel at the top of the stairs and he looked happy to see her.

"I hope you're ready to spend time with me." Samuel's blue eyes were wide as he looked at her. "We haven't spent much alone time today. I've missed my little *fraa.*"

"I've missed seeing you too. The rest of the night is all yours, my precious *ehemann.*"

Samuel's entire face lit up in a smile. "*Wunderbaar.*"

After they were in their bedroom, he pulled her into his arms. He leaned over and kissed her squarely on the mouth...a good long kiss. "How was your day? I missed you at lunch."

"That's Katie's fault. I had to go with her to deliver and serve at a luncheon she catered. I tried to make it up to you by baking your favorite pie today. We can have lunch together tomorrow." She enjoyed their lunches at the bakery as much as Samuel did. The days she worked, they enjoyed eating lunch together. Samuel's furniture store was next door to the Weaver's Bakery and his *mamm* added a lunch menu for him. Sometimes she took a break and watched him making his furniture.

He removed her white *kapp* and took the bobby pins out of her bun. When her long blonde hair fell against her body, he said, "You have such beautiful hair."

While tugging Samuel into her arms, he dropped the pins on the floor. She pressed her lips against his, and he returned her kiss with sweet passion. A shiver of delight went through her as she felt his warm body against hers. Looking up at him, she said shyly, "I'm going to get ready for bed."

He grinned. "Don't take too long."

Later as they snuggled against each other, Rachel murmured, "I love you, Samuel."

"I love you." He kissed her cheek. "I can't wait until spring when I'll start building our house."

"But I thought we were going to wait and stay here longer."

"It'll take time to build even with Peter, my *dat* and Jacob helping me." He chuckled. "Your *dat* might even help. He might be ready to get rid of us. Or me anyhow."

"No, he loves how you help him with the milking in the mornings, so Matthew and Noah can take care of feeding the horses and chickens."

"I thought you'd be happy about getting busy on our own house this spring."

"I guess I'm a bit worried about Judith being here *enough* if we move out."

Samuel gave her shoulder a squeeze. "I don't think it's just about Judith. You've been like a *mamm* to them. I understand that. The boys can visit us a lot at our new house. We won't be far. Remember that's one reason I bought this property because it's close to both our families."

"I'm worried about Judith. What if she loves getting more education and teaching Amish scholars is no longer enough for her? She might decide to leave our way of life. *Daed* will be alone with the boys. I'll feel bad for *Daed* to lose us and Judith in the same year. It'll break his heart." *How things change in a short time,* she thought. *At this time last year I was unhappy with Daed and blamed him for Mamm's death. I thought it was his fault Mamm didn't go to the doctor, and that we didn't have a phone to call in time when she had her heart attack. I was so unhappy that I left Fields Corner. It was the best thing I ever did. Getting away made me realize how wrong I was about everything.*

"This is the best time for Judith to get her GED. After she accomplishes this goal, she might not want additional education."

"I like Eliza but I'm afraid she might influence Judith to want more. I can see her deciding to attend college after she gets her high school diploma."

"Or maybe she'll fall *in lieb* with my *bruder*. Weaver men are hard to resist."

She poked him gently in his side. "Oh, is that right...is that why I married you? I couldn't resist you. Your furniture making talents impressed me the most." She pulled his hand in hers. "No other man has such skillful hands as yours. And not just in your furniture store."

He laughed. "Maybe you should be the writer in the family. You're *wunderbaar* with words."

"*Ya*, maybe I should be." After a quiet and peaceful moment, she said, "I did mention to Judith she could take accounting classes. Bishop Amos won't object to that. She could do the books for Sarah...she's the co-owner of the fabric store."

"Or she could take over for me and do Katie's bookkeeping. I'm glad Katie's catering business is doing well but I wouldn't mind someone else taking care of the books for her."

"That's a great idea. And maybe Judith will be blessed like me and fall *in lieb* with an Amish man...like Jacob. I'm glad Judith's going sledding with Jacob. Has he mentioned getting baptized this year?"

"No, but I think it's good that both he and Judith haven't joined. They don't want to rush into it."

"I hope you're right. All we need is for those two to get wild together and go on their *rumspringa*."

* * *

Judith couldn't sleep because she kept wondering about going sledding with Jacob. Why did he really ask her? *Jacob's handsome and a hard worker,* she thought. Any woman would enjoy being courted by him. Was there a shortage of Amish young women to ask? No young man had shown an interest in her before and asked her to attend anything. She remembered Katie talking about Jacob liking a girl named Leah. That was some time ago.

She sat up in bed when an alarming thought came to her. *Jacob asking me to go sledding must mean he's looking for a future spouse. He's eighteen and has a good job. He hasn't joined the church so maybe he wants to experience the outside world with me and see if we might have enough in common to become serious about each other.*

She twisted a lock of her hair around her finger, wondering if Rachel was still up. She wanted to talk to someone. *I doubt if Rachel will want to talk right now. She left my room to go to bed. I'm sure the two newlyweds won't want to be disturbed by me.* Giggling, she thought, *Samuel's probably showing his appreciation for his butterscotch pie. Nope, I definitely don't want to knock on their bedroom door.*

I should bake something to take to the Sunday get-together. It has to be easy but yummy. If I ask Rachel, she'll offer to bake it. If Mary Zook still attends the Sunday youth activities, she'll be sure to ask me if I baked it myself. Mary probably will go sledding. The only Amish man she'd been interested in had been Samuel. Mary tried her best to get him interested in her, especially when Rachel had gone to Cocoa Beach. She'd practically thrown herself at Samuel from what Katie had told her. I even thought of warning Rachel and writing to her about Mary. Well, she won't try to nab Jacob. He's too young for Mary. I hope she finds the right mate.

After a few minutes of mentally discarding ideas of making cupcakes, cookies, or monkey bread...although Rachel's strawberry monkey bread recipe was good but more difficult to make. And it'd be hard to get fresh strawberries. The grocery store in Fields Corner was small and didn't have the greatest produce department. She remembered the delicious brownies *Aenti* Carrie made for them while at Outer Banks last summer. She told them they were fast and easy to make. Was it too late to call her aunt and get the recipe? And it'd be nice to tell her she was going to get her high school diploma. *Aenti* Carrie had encouraged her to get her GED before joining the church.

She turned the bedside lamp on to see the clock and saw it was nine-thirty. Her aunt was English so stayed up later than they did. It was nice to have an Englisher for a relative, but it had been hard on their mother. *Mamm* missed her only sibling when she moved away to marry *Onkel* Scott. But they were all thankful that *Aenti* Carrie hadn't been baptized so shunning didn't have to occur.

Hopping out of bed, she decided to just put shoes on. She'd grab her winter coat and a flashlight before she went outside to the phone shanty. She was glad to have her flannel pajamas on. Minutes later she checked the answering machine in the shanty, but no messages were left for anyone. After finding the pad with her aunt's phone numbers, she wondered, *Should I call her landline or her cell phone?* She decided to use the landline number.

Her *aenti* answered after a few rings and Judith said, "I hope you weren't sleeping."

"No, I'm just knitting one of my prayer shawls. It's so good to hear your voice but is everything all right?"

"*Ya*, nothing is wrong. I just need to talk to someone and I thought of you." Judith continued in an excited voice, "I have so much to tell you. I had two *wunderbaar* things happen to me today."

Aunt Carrie laughed. "Only two. I'm glad it wasn't more or you might have tried to drive the buggy to Kentucky to tell me. What happened?"

"During my lunch time, Jacob Weaver came to school and asked me to go sledding with him on Sunday. I've never had anyone ask me out for anything."

"I'm sure there have been many boys wanting to date you. You're a wonderful and beautiful young woman. I'm happy that Jacob asked you."

"I want to bake something to take to my first Sunday get-together. Do you think I could make those brownies you made for us on our last visit without messing the recipe up?" She didn't need to explain why she was worried about baking anything; Aunt Carrie had heard about her disastrous attempts at baking and cooking from her *bruders*.

"That's a good choice. I'll give the recipe to you before we hang up. But now I want to hear more about Jacob. Doesn't he work at the lumberyard? I talked to him a little after Rachel and Samuel's wedding. He was very polite and nice."

"*Ya*, he works there." Shivering, she wished it wasn't so cold in the shanty. The buggy blanket she'd grabbed on her way out of the house wasn't helping much.

"What's the second wonderful thing?"

"A college student, Eliza, came and visited our classes today. She wants to be a teacher. She had also asked to interview us for a paper. Ruth thought it'd be better for her to interview me because I'm younger. I'm glad because I really like Eliza. But the best part is she's going to help me study for my GED."

"I'm glad you're going to study for it. I'm sure with your intelligence, Eliza won't need to help you very much." Aunt Carrie cleared her throat. "Is your father okay about this?"

"I haven't told him but he knows I've always been interested in getting my high school diploma. That was the reason I didn't join the church with Rachel," she reminded her aunt.

"I'm proud of you, Judith."

"Enough about me. How are you and Uncle Scott and my cousins?" She heard a long drawn out sigh. "What's wrong?"

"I'm fine but remember how Scott thought about dropping out of politics. Well, he's not going to after all. He plans to run for re-election."

"I'm sorry." When her aunt had fallen in love and married Scott Robinson, he was not in politics. He became interested after they married. Growing up Amish and suddenly being in politics had been a major adjustment for Aunt Carrie.

"Are you calling from the phone shanty? I don't want you to catch cold."

"*Ya*, and it's cold out here. I have my coat over my pajamas and a blanket on my legs but I better get inside. *Danki* for talking with me. I love you."

"I love you too. Oh, let me hurry give you the recipe. And I'll call you on Monday to hear how much fun sledding was with Jacob."

Chapter Five

On Sunday evening, they skated on the pond behind Ruth's barn. Jacob held her hand tightly in his, and said, "You're a superb skater."

Judith laughed merrily. "After a few spills on the ice, I finally remembered how to skate. *Danki* for your patience."

"I was surprised they changed from sledding to skating but this is fun." He grinned. "Are you sure you didn't tell Ruth Yoder that you liked skating better than sledding?"

She shook her head. "I didn't. I looked forward to sledding but I'm glad they decided to go skating instead."

"You know what this means, don't you?" Looking down at her, he grinned.

"I don't have a clue."

"You'll still have to go sledding with me. That was my original invitation."

"Is that right? I might be able to go sledding." Judith smiled at him and felt a rush of pleasure. Secretly, she was relieved that Jacob wanted to spend more time with her. During the whole three hour church service in the morning, she'd had trouble concentrating on the two sermons based on the Book of Acts. *Well, I listened okay to some of the twenty minute one, but during the hour sermon, I was too busy sneaking glances at Jacob.*

She'd been nervous about going to her first youth get-together. Judith was afraid that she'd be boring, and Jacob would be sorry he asked her. But he'd joked and been attentive the whole time. Everyone had been friendly which had surprised her. After graduating from eighth grade, she'd focused on studying to become a teacher. When she turned sixteen, Rachel invited her to go to the Sunday youth singings with her. Judith refused Rachel's invitations. She'd always been an introvert so felt uncomfortable in situations with large groups of people. Teaching was different because Judith loved sharing knowledge with her scholars. She never felt shy in a classroom.

"Judith, your brownies were delicious," Mary Zook yelled, as she whizzed past them.

"*Danki*, Mary. And your monkey bread..." her voice trailed off as she realized Mary was too far away to hear her. "She's a speed skater."

"Maybe we should go get some brownies before they're all gone. Skating made me hungry. I want to get one of my *mamm's* sloppy joe sandwiches too."

I'm glad I used Aenti Carrie's brownie recipe but if we go sledding, I need to learn how to bake something else, Judith thought. *Well, I don't need to worry about recipes right now.* She nodded. "Sloppy joe sandwiches sound great and hot chocolate too. It feels like the temperature is dropping."

After they filled their paper plates with sandwiches, chips, cookies and brownies, they found an empty bench to sit on together.

"Besides skating, what else do you like to do for fun?" Jacob asked.

"I'm afraid it might not sound like fun to you, but I love to read and write. And I enjoy teaching." Taking a deep breath, she continued, "I've never been to a Sunday get-together and I'm glad you invited me. It's been a lot of fun. Rachel's always been more outgoing...like our *mamm* was and I've been shy about attending."

"I'm glad you're having a good time." His gray eyes blinked. "I hope we can do more things together. Would you like to eat pizza on Saturday evening with me? It's *wunderbaar* the pizza is *gut* in our only restaurant in Fields Corner...except for *Mamm's* bakery. "

"I do like pizza. Do I get to choose the toppings?"

He laughed. "As long as they're ones I like too."

"I'm only teasing. I'd like to eat pizza and see you on Saturday."

"I'll come by your place around six."

Mary approached them by their bench, smiling. "You two look cozy. It looks like another Weaver might marry a Hershberger."

Jacob looked surprised at Mary's comment.

"We're just friends," Judith said to fill the silence, wondering why Mary had to mention marriage. "Your monkey bread is yummy."

"*Danki.*" Mary sighed. "I wish I had someone special in my life. As you both know, I liked Samuel but I never had a chance with him. When Rachel went to Florida, I tried hard to get his attention. This is terrible but I even hoped Rachel wouldn't join the church. No wonder I can't get anyone interested in me. I'm not a nice person."

"There's a new Amish man, John, working with me at the lumberyard. I'll introduce you the next time we're eating lunch at the bakery. I think you might like John."

While Jacob spoke with Mary, Judith thought how tall she looked towering over them. Of course, they were seated while Mary stood. But she guessed Mary was close to six feet, so she hoped this John was extremely tall.

Mary perked up. "*Danki*, Jacob. I appreciate that. I hope he'll like me. I'm going to get something to eat and visit with some of my friends. You two enjoy the rest of your evening."

After Mary skated away, Judith said, "That was thoughtful of you to mention someone for Mary. I'll have to admit when she started working at the bakery, I thought about writing Rachel. We all knew Mary wanted the job to be close to Samuel. But Rachel needed to enjoy her time away so I didn't mention Mary in my letter. Besides, I knew she didn't have a chance with Samuel."

Jacob nodded. "Mary was persistent in chasing Samuel, and he kept trying to avoid her. It was hard with working right next to the bakery." He took a bite of his sloppy joe sandwich. "I tried to get Katie interested in John, but she told me that she has no interest in Amish men. She's pouring all her energy into her new catering business. Tim really hurt her when he stopped seeing her."

Katie and Tim had planned on getting married last fall, so it was understandable why Katie Weaver had been crushed when Tim broke up with her because of an English woman. What made it worse was his baptism in their church. Judith sipped her hot chocolate, thinking how Tim's parents would have to shun him for seeing someone out of their faith. Maybe they had already done so. It was all so sad. "Rachel enjoys working with Katie. I was hoping Katie would be here. I only talked to her a little after the church service."

"I told Katie to come tonight but she said no." Jacob stared at her for a moment. "I have a question for you. My boss keeps asking me to get my driver's license so I can help with deliveries. I don't want to upset anyone in my family or others, but started thinking maybe it'd be a good experience to do before I join the church. Do you think your *daed* would still allow us to see each other if I get my driver's license?"

She frowned. "I don't know but I can't see that making him happy. We aren't baptized so technically this is our *rumspringa*. I hope you don't like driving a vehicle so much that you decide to buy a car."

He shook his head. "No, I'll just get my license for work. I'm saving my money so I can buy my own property like Samuel did. I'm not sure yet about getting a license. I'll pray about it more."

Why would Jacob want to buy his own land, she thought. As the youngest son, he'll someday have his parents' place. In many Amish families, the youngest son lived in the main house while the elderly parents eventually moved into the *Grossdaadi Haus.*

"I see your puzzled look about me buying land. I don't see my parents retiring anytime soon. Plus Katie might want the house."

"I hope you can find land at a reasonable price. Maybe you can get a discount on the lumber."

"I hope my boss might give me an employee's discount. I've never asked him."

Leaning closer to Jacob, she thought, *I might as well share my higher education plans with Jacob and see his reaction.* "You aren't the only one thinking of doing something non-Amish during your running around time. I'm going to get my high school diploma. Eliza is a college student at Xavier University in Cincinnati. She's going to help me study so I—"

Ruth Yoder interrupted her and said, "I didn't realize you wanted more education. Does that mean you want to leave our scholars and use your GED to get a job in the English world or go to college? The scholars would miss you and I would too."

Realizing Ruth overheard her plans bothered her. She'd planned on telling her but hadn't wanted to already and seeing Ruth's dismal expression wasn't encouraging. Judith exhaled a deep breath. "I changed my mind about getting baptized with Rachel because I decided to first get my GED. I have no plans to stop teaching at our school. I love being an Amish teacher."

Judith watched her friend, tugging at her black cape hood and drawing it closer to her face. She wore black leather gloves. *I hope my reply appeases Ruth.*

"I've never felt any disadvantage to not having a high school diploma, but you're right to do it before you make a commitment to becoming Amish." Ruth raised her eyebrows. "I hope Eliza only plans to help you study. I'd hate for her to encourage you to do other things that might cause problems with your *dat*. I like Eliza but I hope she remembers we are not of the English world."

* * *

Jacob flicked the reins and said, "Giddy up, Blackie." They took off down the snowy lane as they left Yoders' farm. After a few minutes, he glanced at Judith sitting next to him in his buggy. "Are you warm enough?"

"*Ya*. The heater and blanket are *wunderbaar*. You thought of everything."

"*Gut*. I don't want you getting sick and not able to teach tomorrow." He cleared his throat. "I hope you don't mind me asking but who is this Eliza?"

Judith quickly explained that Eliza had visited the school as a project for one of her classes, since she was studying to become a teacher. "And she interviewed me for an article she's writing for her sociology class."

"She seems very interested in you. How did she happen to decide to come from Cincinnati to visit Fields Corner? It seems like she might have visited any number of schools that would've been closer and English."

Judith shrugged. "I suppose she wanted to learn more about how we teach in our school without any technology. When Eliza was at our house, she asked a lot of questions about our way of life."

Recalling how Rachel had a devious photographer snapping pictures of her while she was on the beach made him wonder if there was more to this Eliza. What if she wanted to publish her paper? As long as she asked permission first and allowed Judith to approve it, then it should be fine. "Did she take pictures...or ask if she could?"

"No, she didn't snap any pictures of anyone. Unless she took one of Minnie."

"Who's Minnie?"

"It's my *bruders'* new pony. Eliza helped name her. But she was dangerous with her iPad and used it to take notes."

He laughed. "Stop. I guess I sounded ridiculous. I know we seem to attract a lot of attention, which is understandable with your uncle being a senator. But I just started thinking how Rachel was exploited when the photographer took pictures of her with Adam's friend, Nick."

Judith was so close her shoulder brushed his. His heart raced at her touch.

"It was terrible the way that photographer took pictures of them like they were a romantic couple and then sold them to the media." She paused for a moment. "I like Eliza and never thought about her being interested in us because of Uncle Scott. She never asked me anything about him. I hope that's not the reason behind her interviewing me."

"It was a different situation. I'm sorry I brought it up. Rachel was with your *aenti* and *onkel* in Florida so of course, a photographer wanted pictures to sell." He noticed her worried look and decided to talk about her getting her high school diploma. *That should be safe,* he thought. "It's great that Eliza's going to help you study. She'll have an easy job. I'm sure you'll pass your GED with flying colors."

"I wonder which one of us will accomplish our goal first. Which do you think is hardest to learn—to study several subjects, or to learn how to drive a truck?"

He rolled his eyes at her. "I think both are hard. I'm not sure I'll get my license yet." *Not too much farther to Judith's house. I wonder if she'll invite me into her house. I'd like to spend a little more time with her.*

"Do you want to get baptized this year? If you do, it's probably not worth it to get your license."

Without any hesitation, he said, "I'm not ready to commit. I think I'll wait until I'm twenty-one. I have a lifetime to be Amish and to follow the rules of the *Ordnung*."

"Did you ever wonder what it would be like if we hadn't been born to Amish parents and instead had English ones?" Judith asked.

"Not really. It's hard for me to imagine not having Amish parents."

"If I'd been born to English parents, I'd have graduated from high school last spring, and I'm guessing I'd be in college instead right now...like Eliza is."

Jacob turned to look at Judith. "Do you want to leave Fields Corner and go to college?"

"Well, I have to first get my high school diploma. I wonder what it'd be like to go to college."

If Judith goes to college, she's not going to join our church. I don't know anyone who's gone to college and returned to get baptized and then become Amish. Sadness went through his mind at the realization that Judith was serious about getting more education. "Suppose you do go to college after you get your GED, what would you like to study?"

"That's just it. I do love teaching so I can't imagine doing something else. But just to have the freedom to go to college would be nice. I can see why some leave our Amish way of life to have more choices and freedom."

"But your *Aenti* Carrie left because she fell in love with an English man. It wasn't because of having a desire for more education, right?"

Judith nodded. "You're right. I don't think she would have left if she hadn't met *Onkel* Scott. I think God meant for her to meet him. I wonder what God wants me to do in life. Does He want me to become Amish or to pursue more education? He brought Eliza into my life for a reason."

As he stopped Blackie in front of Judith's house, he said, "I think you should get your GED and see how you feel after that. Maybe you could take some correspondence courses instead of enrolling in college. If I should have my own business someday, I might take accounting courses."

"*Danki*, Jacob, for listening to me. I'll continue to pray I make the right decisions about my life."

In a gentle voice, he said, "I hope your life might include me. I'd like to be your friend."

"I want to be friends too. I had a *gut* time tonight."

Since Judith seemed to want more freedom, a thought popped in his head. Maybe she'd like to be able to talk to him each day. "Since we both aren't baptized, how about I get cell phones for us? We can talk each day easier that way. I liked being able to talk with you this evening."

He heard her sharp intake of breath. Why did he open his mouth and make such a suggestion? Now she might not want to go out with him again. "It's okay if you don't want to."

"I know a few have cell phones and we are supposed to experience new things in our *rumspringa*, but I'm afraid it might upset my *daed* too much. Mostly he might be afraid it'll be a bad influence on Matthew and Noah. Let me think about it."

"I forgot about your *bruders*. They might decide to ask for cell phones. That wouldn't be good."

"It's getting late so I better let you get home." She smiled. "I'm looking forward to seeing you on Saturday."

Chapter Six

Rachel looked up from the puzzle she was working on with Samuel. Glancing around the room, she asked, "Where's Jacob? Is he still outside?"

"I suppose he's on his way home," Judith said quickly. She apparently had a lot to learn about dating. It never occurred to her to ask Jacob if he wanted to visit with her family. She figured they spent enough time together for a first date. "I didn't realize I should've invited him in."

Shaking her head, Rachel said, "No, you didn't need to. I just thought you might. Did you have a good time?"

Judith nodded. "*Ya*, I did. Jacob asked me out for Saturday. We're going to Pizza Hut."

"Did they eat all the brownies?" Matthew asked as he moved a black checker over one of Noah's red checkers.

Noah groaned. "Pretty soon, you'll have all my checkers."

"My brownies went fast. And Mary Zook told me my brownies were delicious."

"That's *wunderbaar* coming from Mary." Rachel pressed a piece in the puzzle. "She doesn't give out compliments often."

"Mary's a *gut* cook, especially her coffeecake." Samuel touched his stomach. "It hit the spot when she brought it to me in the store. What did she take tonight to the ice skating party?"

Judith laughed at her brother-in-law's teasing. "She took a delicious monkey bread."

Rachel playfully tapped Samuel's arm. "Husband, I remember Mary taking you a piece of coffeecake among other goodies while I was away. *Danki* for the reminder."

David folded his newspaper. "This talk about food is making me hungry."

I better tell Daed my plans to get my high school diploma. It might be better to tell him in front of the whole family...well, almost everyone's here. I can't wait until Peter and Ella are here too. He needs to know before I tell anyone else my plans. Judith sat in a chair by her *daed*.

"How about popcorn?" Rachel asked.

David nodded. "*Ya.* I'd like popcorn but I think Samuel should help you pop it."

Matthew asked, "Could we have grape juice, too, Rachel?"

"*Ya.* If you don't mind going down to the cellar to get it. I'm glad our grapes did well last summer so we have juice and jelly."

"Before everyone rushes off to the kitchen, I want to say something." Judith waited a moment before continuing. "Eliza's going to help me get my GED. *Daed*, this shouldn't be a big surprise because I mentioned wanting more education before *Mamm* died."

David sighed. "Your *mamm* was happy you wanted to teach, but when you told her you wanted more education, she worried about you. She told me how you saw English young women carrying college books. As you know, she didn't approve of you getting more education. Why do you need your GED? Are you planning on leaving Fields Corner to teach in an English school?"

Judith shook her head. Why did everyone think she had some big plans? All she wanted to do was to get her high school diploma. And that wouldn't be enough to teach in a non-Amish school anyhow. "I love teaching my scholars. You don't need to worry. To teach in an English school, I would need a college degree. Getting my high school diploma will satisfy my urge for more education. It doesn't mean I'm going to leave Fields Corner."

David put his reading glasses on the end table by his chair. "Is this the real reason you decided to wait to get baptized?"

"*Ya.* I realized if I got baptized first and then decided to go ahead with getting my high school diploma, I'd be shunned. I couldn't bear to be shunned. I love you all so much."

"Well, even if you were baptized, I'd encourage you to take accounting instead of getting your GED. You're not only good at writing, but you're smart in math. Bishop Amos respects the desire to get more education if it will help Amish businesses."

Not this accounting topic again, Judith thought. "I don't want to take accounting. I want to get my high school diploma."

David gave her a thoughtful look. "You've been *froh* teaching in our small Amish school...so I have to wonder if this college student, Eliza Dunbar, put this in your head to get your diploma."

"She's offered to help me study for it. But the desire to learn was put in me by God. He created me."

Rachel cleared her throat. "If Judith doesn't get her GED now, I'm afraid she'll always regret it."

"I don't approve because if you plan to eventually join the church, then you don't need a diploma." In a gruff voice, her *daed* said, "Keep praying about it. Maybe you'll get some sense and realize it's a waste of time."

"I've been praying about it for years." At this remark, she saw how disappointed her father looked. *I always wanted his approval. Daed was the reason I waited to go ahead with studying for my GED. I'm glad Eliza gave me the push I needed to do this.*

David stood. "I'll get the grape juice but I don't want any popcorn. I think I'll go to bed."

Judith hated seeing her father unhappy about her decision, but she was glad she spoke about it to him. If Eliza came to their house to help her study, she didn't want to do it in secret. Ever since she was eight years old, a special bond existed between them. During this time, her *daed* spent a lot of time with her while she recovered in the hospital from double pneumonia. Her *mamm* stayed home with her twin baby brothers, and teenager Peter milked the cows.

I wish Daed could have found it in his heart to give me his approval. How could more education be a waste of time? I'll still study for it but some of the excitement's gone now. Judith watched her *dat* leave the room and felt sad that he couldn't understand why she wanted more from life than an eighth grade education.

But she was even more surprised at Ruth's reaction. Her fellow teacher assumed the same thing as *Daed* — that she might not stay to teach in their Amish school. Well, at least Ruth hadn't told her to forget about getting her high school diploma.

Noah stood by her side. "It's okay, Judith. When Matthew and I make *Daed* angry, he gets over it."

Matthew said, "He might give you extra chores to do to punish you."

She smiled at her lovable *bruders*. "*Danki* for the advice."

"It's *gut* you had fun with Jacob." Noah looked serious. "If you two get married, will Jacob live here too?"

She laughed. "I only went out with Jacob once so it's too early to mention marriage."

From the kitchen, Rachel yelled, "Popcorn's ready. Come and get it."

After the boys left to get popcorn and grape juice, Judith remembered Jacob asking if Eliza took any pictures. It never occurred to her that Eliza had some ulterior motive for interviewing her. But was that why she offered to help her study? Eliza did mention her brother writing for a newspaper. She exhaled a breath of relief. If Eliza knew about her famous *onkel* and *aenti*, she wouldn't let it slip her brother wrote for the media. Or would she?

Was Eliza helping her study so she could get more information about her popular Uncle Scott?

* * *

After taking care of Blackie for the night, Jacob entered the Weaver's house and saw his sister Katie and his *mamm* at the kitchen table. He hung his coat and hat on the hooks by the door.

Katie stopped adding figures on her calculator. "Do you know any Englisher who might like to make some extra money? My driver, Joan, quit today."

He shrugged. "I can't think of anyone right now."

"If you do let me know as soon as possible. Joan's going to continue for two more weeks, and then she needs to quit. Her husband retired and he's not well. She doesn't want to leave him alone."

"That's too bad. Joan's a nice lady." Jacob grinned at Katie. "What if I get my driver's license? I can drive you when I'm not working at the lumberyard or helping *Daed* with the farm."

"That's not a *gut* idea," Martha put her cup of tea on the table. "I know this is your *rumspringa* but I don't want you to drive a car. I'm afraid you might be in a terrible accident. I heard in the bakery the other day how five teenagers were killed in an automobile accident. They ran a stop sign."

"Terrible buggy accidents happen to Amish too. Judith's grandparents were killed in their buggy by a teenager. That doesn't mean I'll be careless. Mike has asked me to get my license so I can make deliveries for him." He removed a glass from the cabinet before continuing. "I told him no but maybe I should."

"You won't be able to get baptized if you have a driver's license," Katie said.

"I still plan on getting baptized but not for a couple of years." Jacob poured a glass of milk before sitting in a chair next to his mother. "I'd like to help Mike out with the deliveries before I become Amish. He's been good to me and is understanding whenever I need to take time off to help on the farm."

"I don't like it. I know your *dat* won't either." Martha patted his arm. "But I'm *froh* to hear you want to get baptized."

"For two years we can have a free driver." Katie grinned at him. "Okay, I can't stand it any longer. How was the big evening with Judith?"

"We had fun. We're going to Pizza Hut on Saturday." He took a drink of milk. "I'm a bit worried because she's going to get her GED. I hope she'll still be interested in seeing me."

Katie removed her white prayer covering. "I can see why that worries you, but she's already smarter than you anyhow. Let's face it...women are smarter than men."

Jacob laughed. "Don't let *Daed* or Samuel hear you say that."

"Irene worried about Judith leaving our community. Judith told her she wanted to go to college." Martha arched her eyebrows. "Irene would be *froh* you two are seeing each other. I know I am. You might be the reason Judith will stay with us."

"That's another reason I want to drive trucks for Mike. I'll make more money. I want to buy some land to build a house."

"I can't believe you and Samuel both think you have to build a new house." Martha frowned. "You can live here after you marry. Your father and I were disappointed Samuel bought land so he can build a house. We hoped that he and Rachel would live here. We have plenty of room."

"If I and my bride decide to live here, we'll still need money." He didn't want to mention Katie might want the house for herself someday.

Martha waved a finger at him and Katie. "Money isn't everything. You both make sure you don't make money your priority in life. God must be first."

"I have to be concerned about making a living. I'm not going to have a husband." Katie exhaled a deep breath. "I know I didn't have to start a business, but it's kept me from crying my eyes out over Tim's rejection. Katie's Catering has given me a purpose in life since I don't have a wedding to look forward to now."

Martha leaned across the table and squeezed Katie's hand. "You're young and will still meet someone."

Katie shook her head and looked sadly at them. "I don't see that happening. I was sure Tim was the right man for me. I don't want to marry someone else."

Should I tell Katie about the bishop's son, Luke? I like Luke and think he might be interested in Katie. "What about Luke King? I saw him looking at you today after the church service."

Katie looked surprised. "Why would he be interested in me? He's seeing someone from another district."

Jacob shook his head. "He isn't now. She left to visit relatives in Michigan. He seemed glad she went away."

"Maybe Luke's the man for you," Martha said eagerly.

Katie didn't look convinced. "I wonder if Bishop Amos would approve of me for his son. Besides, I already told you I wasn't interested in John and I still feel the same way about Amish men. I hope you don't break Judith's heart like Tim did mine."

"I don't plan on hurting Judith."

"Did you see Samuel and Rachel when you took Judith home?" Martha asked.

Jacob shook his head and frowned. "I was disappointed she didn't invite me inside." *I won't mention I might have irritated her when I brought up her onkel could be the reason Eliza was interested in being her friend.*

"Judith's shy so I'm sure that's why she didn't. She'll invite you inside soon," Martha said, standing. "I'm going up to bed."

"*Gut nacht, Mamm,*" he said.

Katie took their cups. "I'll rinse our cups. We can use them in the morning for our coffee. Hope you sleep well."

Once their mother was out of their kitchen, Katie said, "Are you serious about getting your driver's license? I'll pay you to drive and a lot of my catering jobs are on Saturdays and in the evening so you can still work at the lumberyard."

"I don't know what to do. This is the time for me to do it. I don't want to upset Judith's *daed*. Do you think he'll be upset if I get my license and he'll tell Judith not to see me?"

"You really do like Judith a lot. I'm glad. I can see her being my future sister-in-law." Katie chuckled. "She might even learn how to cook. If she doesn't, she can do my sewing and I'll prepare meals so you won't starve."

"Her brownies were delicious tonight. Mary Zook even complimented her."

"I bet Rachel baked them."

"No, I'm sure Judith did." He finished drinking his glass of milk. "I'll pray about the whole driving situation. But I won't be able to drive you unless I have a vehicle. I'm not planning on buying a car. I'm just going to drive truck for Mike if I decide to get my license."

Katie smoothed her apron. "I didn't even think about that. If God wants me to continue with my catering business, the right driver will come along. And you do what you feel is right for your life. *Gut nacht*, Jacob."

What is right for me, he wondered, after Katie went to bed. *Should I get my driver's license? I'd like to drive but I don't want to worry my parents. I definitely don't want to cause any friction between Judith and her dat by getting my license. Being with Judith was great. I don't think I can wait until Saturday to see her again. Maybe I'll go to the school to see her during my lunch time.*

"Oh, please, don't tell me your eyes are all dreamy over Judith," Katie said, upon entering the kitchen. "Another Weaver man smitten by a Hershberger woman. I don't believe it."

"I thought you went to bed."

"I came back to get my calculator."

"You're right. I've been crazy about Judith for a long time but just kept it to myself."

"She must like you. You got her to go ice skating. Rachel and I've been trying to get Judith to go to Sunday singings for a long time."

Maybe Judith liked him even though he had no desire to get a high school diploma. He smiled at Katie. "You're right. She must like me."

Chapter Seven

"It's good to be back visiting your school." Eliza smiled at Judith as she entered the classroom.

"*Danki* you again for the beautiful flowers. They definitely brighten a dreary day." Judith touched the vase of brilliant pink flowers on her desk.

She'd dropped off flowers the first thing in the morning for Judith before leaving to sit in on Ruth's classes. "You're very welcome. I wanted to show my appreciation for you and Ruth letting me observe your classes. I'm happy to be here for your afternoon classes. The morning seemed long while I observed Ruth's teaching methods." *Should I mention to Judith how uncomfortable I was in Ruth's classroom?*

"Oh, do you regret coming for the whole day this time?" Judith asked.

Sitting in a front desk close to Judith's desk, Eliza shrugged and turned her head to look out the window. "I want to make sure Ruth's outside with the scholars." She saw Ruth talking with a an older student so turned back to Judith. "Good, she's not around so I can talk. I sensed a difference in Ruth's attitude this morning. I thought about wearing a dress instead of pants, but I wore pants last week. I guess I stick out in my clothing here." *Maybe I shouldn't say anything to Judith but Ruth's coolness was apparent. Could I have offended Ruth in some way?* Eliza wondered.

Judith sighed. "I'm afraid it's because you're going to help me study for my GED test. I went ice skating with Jacob at Ruth's place, and she overheard me talking about getting my high school diploma. She doesn't seem to think it's a wise decision on my part."

Eliza's eyes widened. "I don't understand why a teacher would be against another teacher getting more education? Ruth should be thrilled instead. Do you think she's jealous because she doesn't have her GED?"

Judith shook her head. "I don't think she's jealous. She seems to feel the same way as my *daed*...that if I'm going to continue to teach here, it's pointless to get my high school diploma. My *daed* suggested I take accounting courses because that would be acceptable to our faith. Bishop Amos doesn't mind if we take accounting if it's to help us with our businesses."

"Wow, I'm sorry I've caused problems for you with your dad and Ruth. Would it be better for you if I didn't help you study for your GED?" Eliza stared at Judith to see her reaction to the question.

As Judith fingered her *kapp's* ties, she said, "I want your help and I appreciate you doing this for me. My *daed* and Ruth mentioned that you might influence me with your English ways. They even said something about me leaving Fields Corner to teach in an English school. Getting my high school diploma doesn't mean I'm leaving to go elsewhere."

Should I even mention going to a college class with me? I thought maybe Judith could be a guest speaker and tell what it's like to be Amish. I won't mention the speaking part. "I was going to see if you would want to attend a class or two with me but now it seems that might be a bad idea." Eliza grinned at Judith. "You might influence me to become Amish. I was thinking how interesting it would be for us to switch places when I was driving home last week."

Judith grinned back at her and laughed. "I can't see you in Amish clothes. And by the way, you are dressed fine to observe our classroom. You look pretty in your pants and sweater. We're used to seeing English tourists all the time in our town. I'd better wait on going to a class with you."

"I understand, but hope you can sometime. I'd like you to experience a college class. I think you'd enjoy it."

Judith seemed troubled. "My *daed* told me how my *mamm* worried about me after I told her how I saw women carrying college books, and I wanted more education. She was proud of me becoming a teacher, but definitely didn't want me to get more than an eighth grade education. I think that's a reason why I haven't pursued getting my diploma. You came into my life at just the right time."

"Have you used a laptop or any computer before? If you take your test by the end of this year, you can still take a paper test. But after this year, Ohio is changing to applicants only taking the test on computers." *I doubt Judith has used a computer but I could be wrong,* Eliza thought.

Judith nodded. "I used my *Aenti* Carrie's at their beach house last summer. Of course, *Daed* and the boys were gone the few times I used it."

Eliza leaned closer to Judith's desk. "It'd be great if I could call you to see if you have any questions. After hearing how your father and Ruth aren't on board about you getting your GED, I'd rather not leave messages here or at your phone shanty. I can buy a cheap cell phone for you and we'll just call when necessary. What do you think?"

Judith blinked. "I can't believe this. You're the second person to mention me having a cell phone. Jacob, Samuel's younger brother, mentioned getting cell phones so we can talk to each other. I told him my *daed* might think it would be a bad influence because of my *bruders*. But Jacob made a good argument that we're not baptized. This is the time for us to try new things during our *rumspringa*."

Could Jacob be Judith's boyfriend? She never mentioned him before but it'd be interesting to hear more about their dating traditions if he should be. "Is Jacob someone special in your life?"

"We're friends and have known each other for a long time with our two families being close. He came last

Tuesday during my lunch before you came and invited me to go sledding...except the youth get-together was changed to ice skating." Judith looked shy, all of a sudden. "He asked me out for this Saturday to go to Pizza Hut."

"I hope you said yes."

Judith nodded. "I'm looking forward to seeing him again."

"Well, this might be a good time for you to have your own phone. You can call me if you want to ask me anything and then you could also talk with Jacob. It's a win-win situation." Now that she mentioned the cell phone, Eliza wondered if it'd be a problem for Judith to charge it. It was funny how having electricity was so commonplace for her, so she kept forgetting how using modern devices would be difficult for Judith. "Would you have a problem charging your phone?"

"I'll ask my English neighbor, Sharon Maddox, if I can charge it at her house. She won't mind. My *mamm* and Sharon were close friends."

"I'm glad you can charge it there."

"I'll think about it and let you know before you go home today." Judith smiled. "I'm glad you're coming for supper this evening. Rachel and the boys are thrilled too."

Judith had invited her to eat with them when she'd delivered the flowers in the morning. "After school I want to stop and buy the dessert for supper," Eliza said. "I called Rachel this morning, and told her I'd like to contribute to the meal."

"*Danki.* But you don't need to do that."

"It's the least I can do."

"But you're my tutor now so you're already doing a lot for me."

"I'm hoping to ace my sociology and education courses this semester because of your interview...and because you and Ruth have allowed me to observe."

"Well, I hope you get an A in each class."

Eliza grinned. "By the way, one reason I wore pants was because I thought it might be your turn to do recess duty. I planned on playing with the kids. I offered to go outside with Ruth, but she told me to see if you wanted me to help with teaching this afternoon."

"Sure, you can listen to the first and second graders read while I spend time with the third and fourth graders." Judith pointed to a corner. "I take them there and they sit on chairs in a small circle to read out loud to me. We have some good readers. I don't think I mentioned to you that the Amish learn to speak English when they start school. It's a second language to us."

"I didn't know that."

Judith smiled. "We speak Pennsylvania Dutch at home but it didn't originate in the Netherlands. Although there's some uncertainty over the origin of the term, the 'Dutch' description has been considered an Anglicized version of 'Deutsch'."

"Maybe you can teach me to speak Amish."

Judith laughed. "I guess if we switch places like you mentioned, it would be an good idea for you to learn to speak our language."

I wonder if I could receive extra credit for learning to speak Pennsylvania Dutch. Turning her head so she could see the window, Eliza watched the children playing outside. "Do they speak English while on the playground or do they use Pennsylvania Dutch?"

"They use English mostly but with a few Pennsylvania Dutch words sprinkled in their conversations. Like I do." Judith paused for a moment. "I don't have recess duty today because Ruth and I rotate. This month I have it on Monday, Wednesday, and Friday. The funny thing is these particular days have been the coldest days, so I've been taking them to the basement to play. That's right, I just realized—you've never seen our basement." Glancing at the wall clock, Judith commented, "We have a few minutes before the children come inside. I'll show it to you now."

"I'd love to see the basement." Eliza stood and followed Judith to the hallway. "That's probably why Ruth told me Tuesday was a good day to visit. She wanted to give us time since I'm interviewing you." *I hope Ruth doesn't regret suggesting I interview Judith instead of her,* Eliza thought.

Once they were in the basement, Judith pointed to the Ping-Pong table. "Ping-Pong is popular with the older students when we have recess inside. The younger children like to play Duck Duck Goose. Some like to do draw pictures. Board games are popular too."

"The basement is huge and perfect for the days you have to stay in." Eliza noticed several pictures of animals on one of the walls. She moved closer to take a better look. "You have some artistic scholars."

Judith smiled. "These were all done by one special student. Take a guess who the artist is."

"It must be someone I know, so I bet it's Noah. He seems to be sensitive and creative from what I've observed."

Judith nodded. "Excellent guess. Noah definitely is talented in art. He drew Minnie already but he hasn't put the drawing on the wall here yet. He'll have to show it to you."

Eliza saw a sad expression cross Judith's face. "Minnie isn't sick, is she?"

Judith shook her head and exhaled a deep breath. "No, Minnie's fine. I just thought about something else Noah drew last week. He drew our mother. Rachel saw it first and she told me. The problem is we aren't allowed to have faces show in our drawings or pictures."

"I didn't know you weren't allowed to have pictures of faces."

"Our *Aenti* Carrie gave a picture of our sweet *mamm* to me and to Rachel. She decided to wait until the boys were older. They might let it slip and we don't want to get in trouble with Bishop Amos. Anyhow Noah's picture is beautiful. He did it all from memory."

"I guess I can't take a picture of you then." Eliza wanted to have one with her paper. Maybe she could snap it from the side so Judith's face wouldn't show as much.

Judith grinned. "I can't pose but you can snap it of me. If you ask me for permission before you take it, I have to refuse."

"It seems like since you aren't baptized, it should be okay."

"Bishop Amos speaks about "graven images" a lot and how it's unacceptable to have pictures of ourselves and it shows pride if we do." Judith shrugged. "Rachel thinks since *Mamm's* passed on that it shouldn't hurt for Noah to have a drawing of her. But we haven't told *Daed* yet."

"I won't take any pictures," Eliza said, "I don't want to cause you any trouble."

Judith gave her a thoughtful look. "Oh no. Is there something else I should know?"

"Talking about pictures made me think of something Jacob brought up on Saturday evening when we talked about you helping me study for my GED...but we better go back to the classroom. I hear the children upstairs. I'll tell you about it after school."

As they went up the stairs, Eliza thought, *What would Jacob mention that concerns me?*

* * *

After supper they went to Judith's bedroom. Eliza removed a folder from her bag, setting it on a desk. She ran her fingers over the cherry wood, staring for a minute at the desk. "This is a beautiful desk. I love all the drawers. Whoever made this does fantastic work. Did Samuel make it?"

"No, my Grandpa Troyer made it for my fifteenth birthday. It's even more special to me since he's gone. He and my grandmother died a couple months before my *mamm's* death."

"I'm sorry he and your grandmother died too. It was so sad a car hit their buggy."

How does Eliza know my grandparents were killed in a road accident? I've never mentioned it to her. Did Noah and Matthew tell her? "*Danki.* How did you know they were in a buggy accident?"

"I saw it on the TV news." Eliza opened the folder. "I printed off a GED study guide and practice tests for you."

Maybe Eliza lied about her reason to interview me for her college class. I teased Jacob when he wondered why Eliza was so interested in me. It could be because of my onkel being a well-known senator. Jacob's implication might be on target about Eliza. Judith shivered when a chill suddenly went through her body. "You didn't just happen to decide to visit our Amish school, did you? It's because you knew about my famous Uncle Scott, isn't it?"

Eliza gave her a startled look. "I became interested in your way of life because of the news story about your grandparents. It got my attention and I thought how sad it was they were killed. I admit I knew about your aunt and uncle before I called Ruth, but I'm not here to use you in any way to get information about them. I'm only interested in what I told you I'm writing for my classes. I have never planned on writing anything about your aunt and uncle."

Judith sat on the edge of her bed and fiddled with the hem of her dress. "Jacob reminded me how a photographer took pictures of Rachel on the beach. The photographer sold the pictures and an article about Rachel and implied there was a romance between her and Nick, a friend of our cousin's."

"My brother, Austin, told me about those pictures. I hadn't seen them but I mentioned to him I was going to observe your school. I'm sorry the photographer took advantage of Rachel. I promise I won't do that. I thought about taking a picture of you to put with my college paper but I won't. When you mentioned that your faith doesn't believe in having pictures of people, I already decided not to take one of you."

I wonder if I can believe Eliza. Maybe I shouldn't depend on Eliza to help me study. She crossed her arms in front of her chest. "Jacob asked why you chose our school to visit when there were closer ones to where you live. I had to ask you because my *daed* knew it wasn't Rachel's fault that the photographer snapped pictures of her, but this is a different situation. I've invited you into our home so I just don't feel comfortable with you helping me study for the GED. My *daed's* already unhappy enough about me getting my diploma. I'm thinking it might be better if I study on my own. You have to drive too far, but we can finish the interview this evening." She hadn't meant to get upset, but she regretted now having Eliza tutor her. *What was I thinking? I can do this on my own.*

"Judith, I'm happy to help you study. I don't mind driving here. I love your family. Even though we just met, you're already my friend. I'm sorry. I should've told you last week that I knew your uncle was a senator. Austin told me to tell you right away, but I was afraid you'd think I was interviewing you for some other purpose. I'm not. I swear to you I'm not. I want to help you study. I don't need to observe your class again. I met the hour requirement for my education class since I stayed the whole day. If you get a cell phone, you can call me with questions so that'll cut down the driving time. But I enjoy visiting and my mom wants to see the stores in Fields Corner so I plan on bringing her sometime."

"I'll get a cell phone. I'll call you with any questions. I'd like to meet your mother so I hope you bring her to visit."

Eliza leaned closer and touched Judith's hand. "I'd like you to visit one of my classes. No one has to know who you are. I know you'd enjoy experiencing a college class."

"I think my Plain clothing might be a giveaway about my identity." Judith gave a slight laugh. "I don't know about going to one of your classes, but maybe sometime I could visit your college campus." *But I'll have to keep that visit to myself. No need to upset Daed.*

Eliza laughed. "No rush. I'll be in college for awhile."

"We better get busy." Judith sat on the chair and continued, "You have a long drive home. I appreciate everything you're doing for me, but I had to question you. I'm sorry if I was rude, but your world seems to have a huge fascination with anything related to our way of life. I don't want to cause anymore anxiety for my *daed*."

Rachel entered the room, carrying a plate of cookies. "I brought you two scholars a snack to enjoy while you study. Eliza, *danki*, for buying the carrot cake and these cookies."

"You're welcome, Rachel." Eliza frowned at Judith. "I don't want to cause your father any anxiety. I promise I won't take pictures of you or your family."

"What's this about *Daed's* anxiety?" Rachel asked.

Judith shrugged. "Eliza and I talked about *Onkel* Scott and how the photographer sold pictures of you when you were in Florida. We would have to have a famous senator in the family. If we were English, no one would be interested in us being his nieces."

"Or if he left politics that would be *wunderbaar* but instead I'm afraid he might run for president. I was with *Onkel* Scott and *Aenti* Carrie in Florida so that didn't help any. At least, no one knew about our summer visit to Outer Banks so the media didn't bother any of us." Rachel set the plate on the desk.

Judith took an oatmeal raisin cookie. "It was sweet of you to buy an assortment of cookies for us, too, Eliza." She felt a tinge of guilt at questioning Eliza, but glad she did. Eliza's answers had convinced her that she could believe her new friend.

Running her fingers over the ties of her prayer *kapp*, Rachel said, "*Daed* needs something else to think about. We should invite Sarah and her daughter to come to supper some evening."

"Or you could get pregnant, so *Daed* could think about being a *grossdaddi*." Judith grinned at Rachel.

"And you could think about being an *aenti* instead of getting your GED."

"Don't say that. I need your support." *I hope Rachel's not serious,* Judith thought.

"I'm still in your corner, but I couldn't resist teasing you. I've been hoping Ella and Peter will be blessed with a *boppli*." Rachel exhaled a deep breath. "I look forward to having lots of *kinner*, but it'll be hard not having *Mamm* with us. She would've made a *wunderbaar grossmammi*."

Judith swallowed a bite of cookie. "I'll invite Sarah tomorrow after school for Thursday evening. We can't have her Friday because after school we're making subs for a fundraiser for the Kline family. You're still going to help, right?"

Rachel said, "*Ya*, I wouldn't miss it. Katie's helping too."

Eliza said in a rush, "Oh, I wish I could help. I'm scheduled to work at the hospital. Maybe I could switch with someone."

I don't think Eliza better come again on Friday. Daed won't be happy if she comes too often. He'll worry I won't join the Amish faith. Life seems to be complicated when you have an English friend. "That's okay, don't change your schedule. We have plenty of help. Another time you might be free to help. None of us have medical insurance so we always help one another out when necessary."

"I better leave so you two can work," Rachel said.

After Rachel left the room, Eliza said, "I'll tell you first about the application process. Before taking your GED test, you must first complete and submit your online GED application online. The application can no longer be downloaded from their website. You can pay for your test online with a credit card, or you can download the confirmation page and mail it with your payment."

"I don't have a credit card so I'll have to mail it with a check."

"I can bring my laptop sometime and we can go somewhere where there's Internet for you to do your application. I know you mentioned using your aunt's computer, but I'll be happy to help you register using my laptop."

"*Danki*, Eliza. I'll need help because it's been months since I used a computer. I never got on the Internet by myself. My cousin Violet helped me with the computer."

Chapter Eight

"This is so nice not to have to cook. *Danki* for inviting us to supper. Everything is delicious." Sarah Miller smiled across the table at Rachel and Judith.

Judith smiled back. "I'm glad you and Abigail could come. I miss having Abigail in class since she moved to Miss Yoder's classroom." *I just hope Daed takes an interest in Sarah. If he's busy seeing her, he might not be as stressed about me studying for my GED,* Judith thought.

"We want to show Abigail our new pony, Minnie." Noah jabbed his fork into a mound of mashed potatoes and gravy.

"Eliza helped us choose a name for her," Matthew said.

"Who's Eliza?" Abigail asked.

"She's a college student. Eliza's helping Judith study for a big high school test," Noah said in a rush.

Sarah's eyebrows shot up. "Is it the GED test?"

Judith nodded, avoiding looking at her *daed*. Why did this topic have to come up, she wondered, feeling anxious at the very thought of even talking about her education plan in front of her father. "I want to get my high school diploma before I join the church."

"I can't believe it. I did the same thing." Sarah tucked a loose strand of black hair back under her *kapp* before continuing. "Well, there's more. My husband wanted me to get my GED. It wasn't that important to me at the time but I'm glad I did now."

"Why did you husband want you to get your GED?" David gave an embarrassed glance at Sarah. "If you don't mind me asking."

Sarah's brown eyes widened as she looked across the table at David. "I don't mind at all. I was eighteen when I married Henry and I was ready to have a family with him. But I never had Abigail until I was twenty-seven and before this happened, it bothered me greatly that God hadn't blessed us with *bopplin*. I think Henry wanted to give me something else to occupy my mind, and he suggested I get my GED. He helped me study for it."

Whew, Judith thought. *I'm glad Sarah said this so Daed will realize some Amish men don't think it's terrible for a woman to get a bit more education.*

"That seems unusual for an Amish husband," Rachel said.

Samuel frowned. "I don't think it is. I'd encourage you as long as it wasn't against our *Ordnung.*"

Sarah cleared her throat. "He wasn't Amish but Mennonite. I met him before I became Amish. My parents didn't give their blessing at first, but I'm their only child and they finally accepted my marriage." Sarah squeezed her daughter's hand. "They adore Abigail."

Stunned and speechless, Judith glanced at her father to see his reaction to Sarah's news. A few in their community had left their way of life to go to the Mennonite churches. *Daed* never understood why they would make a commitment, then disobey their *Ordnung* when they'd be shunned by their Amish family and friends.

"So what are you now?" Matthew asked.

Sarah laughed. "You get right to the point. That's *gut*, Matthew. I'm Amish. I was baptized six years ago."

"Your husband must have been a special man for you to leave your Amish community."

Judith noticed her *daed* gave Sarah an intense glance with his comment. *Maybe he'll still be interested in Sarah, even though she left our Plain life to marry a non-Amish man.*

"He was a special man. Henry was a *gut* husband and *daed*." Sarah stared back at David. "He died while waiting for a kidney transplant."

"I'm sorry your husband died. Our *mamm* died from a heart attack." Noah exhaled a deep breath. "We loved her a lot but God still took her."

"I'm sorry about your mother." Sarah stopped buttering a piece of bread. "I've heard from many people how loved she was in Fields Corner. I know how hard it is to go on when we lose someone so close to us, but God wants us to continue with our lives."

"That's right. God knows best even though it's hard to accept at times." Rachel took a sip of her coffee. "*Mamm* wants us to be happy."

"We've both lost a spouse." David's voice dropped as he continued, "I know it was God's will but each day I wish Irene was still alive."

Sarah's brown eyes filled with compassion. "Losing Irene the way you did was a shock. I knew Henry might die if he didn't get a transplant in time, but still it was all painful when he passed. God will continue to give you strength and peace." Sarah glanced around the table at everyone. "Lean on your family. My parents' support helped us through a rough time."

"I feel blessed to have *wunderbaar* children...and a daughter who cooks like her mother." David smiled at Rachel before taking a bite of chicken.

While she was a Mennonite, Sarah might have driven a car. *Obviously, she couldn't drive now so had it been difficult for her to quit driving a car and switching back to a horse and buggy?* Judith sat up straighter in her chair. "Sarah, I hope you don't mind me asking, but did you ever get your driver's license?"

Her *daed* looked surprised at her question. But she worried if Jacob got his driver's license that he might not want to join their church, Judith thought. Samuel and his family wouldn't be happy, but more importantly, she wasn't sure Jacob should drive a truck for his boss.

Sarah nodded. "I did get my license but I didn't drive a car often. Mostly, when we needed groceries. And I drove Henry to his doctor appointments and for his dialysis treatments."

"I know someone who's thinking of getting a driver's license before being baptized. It's for work and I wonder if that might cause my friend to want to continue driving." Judith noticed Samuel frowning. *I should have kept quiet. I hope he doesn't ask if my friend is Jacob. I don't want Daed to be upset about Jacob wanting to get his license.*

Matthew asked Abigail, "Would you like to see Minnie now?"

Abigail leaned closer to her mother. "*Mamm*, is it okay if I go see Minnie?"

"*Ya.* Put your plate and glass by the sink before you go."

Abigail stood and pushed her chair in. "*Danki* for inviting us and supper was *gut.*"

* * *

Rachel sat on a deep green upholstered chair in Judith's room. "Even though things didn't go as planned, I'm glad we had Sarah and Abigail over tonight."

"I still can't believe how fast *Daed* left after dessert to read the newspaper."

Rachel shrugged. "Sarah mentioned having us over sometime. Maybe he'll go when she invites us."

"That might be a possibility to get them together again. But otherwise we might have to eliminate Sarah as a future wife for *Daed*. In the past, he's complained about a few Amish leaving to go to the Mennonite church." Judith sighed. "It's hard to believe that Sarah was married to a Mennonite, but I guess with her living in a different district than ours, we don't know as much about her as we thought. We assumed she was married to an Amish man."

Removing her prayer *kapp*, Rachel nodded. "But at least she hadn't been baptized when she married a non-Amish man. Maybe it's for the best. It might too soon for *Daed* to think about getting married. *Mamm* and he were married for a long time. I want him to be happy, but at the same time it'd be hard to see *Daed* with a new wife."

"He might never have a place in his heart for another woman. It'd be hard to replace *Mamm*. If it ever happens, I'd rather it'd be Sarah than Barbara."

Rachel laughed a little. "Can you believe Sarah has her high school diploma? Here we were trying to avoid the GED topic in front of *Daed* and instead we ended up talking about it."

"It could be a *gut* thing, though." Judith kicked her black shoes off and plopped down on her bed. "Sarah's Amish and has her high school diploma. *Daed* might come to the conclusion that it's not a bad thing for me to get mine."

"That's true. Sarah's having her GED might have helped when she opened her store. If she had to get a bank loan, I'm sure it helped give her creditability. And *Daed* might realize you aren't going to leave us to get a college education. He might see that getting your diploma will be a positive thing in your life." Rachel leaned closer and grasped her hand for a moment. "At least, I hope it will be and you won't leave us to live in the English world."

Judith laughed. "Do you realize we had a similar conversation before you left for Florida? I was afraid you might decide to become English."

"We did, that's right. I suppose we'll have the same conversation again with Matthew and Noah. I can see Noah questioning our Amish beliefs. It's *gut* we're allowed to experience different things before we make the decision to commit to the Plain way of life." Rachel's expression became thoughtful. "It seems to me that *Daed's* more upset about you getting your high school diploma than he was about me leaving home."

Judith shook her head. "No, he was concerned a lot about you. It was a difficult time for him. I think that was the main reason I thought about getting baptized with you...to make him happy that both his daughters were joining the church. But I couldn't and realized it wasn't the right time for me to commit." *I wonder if I ever will be ready to accept the rules of the Ordnung. The English are fortunate in that way because they don't have to make such a big decision whether to accept such a restrictive lifestyle. So much is not allowed for us—no college education, many careers are off limits in the Plain community, no computers, no electricity, no phones...but also it's good there aren't as many distractions in the Amish world because it helps us to have a deeper relationship with the Lord.*

"So what are you going to wear on your date with Jacob?"

She smiled at her sister. "Maybe I'll go casual and wear jeans and a bright red sweater."

"Okay, smart one. Which dress are you going to wear? Although wearing English clothes would definitely get Jacob's attention."

"And our father's attention. I thought I'd wear my lavender one." *Should I tell Rachel about Jacob getting cell phones for us? Probably should, it might come in handy if we ever have an emergency and we can't get to our phone in the shanty. Plus she's going to see it anyhow when she comes into my bedroom.*

"Good choice. I like that color on you." Rachel yawned. "I guess I better get to bed. And I know you have a busy day tomorrow too."

"Before you leave, I need to tell you something important. Jacob asked me about getting a cell phone during our *rumspringa* and at first, I didn't think it was a good idea. But Eliza mentioned it, too, so it would be easier for us to talk on the phone when I have questions about any subject I'm studying."

"I mentioned to Samuel about getting a cell phone." Rachel loosened her bun and her blonde hair fell past her shoulders. "It'd be handy for a medical emergency. And in another Amish district, the bishop gave permission to business owners to have them. But Samuel doesn't like cell phones. He thinks they invade home life too much when teenagers have them during their *rumspringa*. I told him they're only to be used for medical or business purposes. And in your case, it'll save time. You can be studying and talk to Eliza with your questions instead of running to the phone shanty. *Ya*, it's a *gut* idea."

"I'm glad I have your support because I talked to Jacob

today and he's going to get them. They won't be the fancy iPhones but just basic cell phones. He said they are pretty cheap and we won't get a phone plan or anything."

"I'm glad you're seeing Jacob. I better leave now so you can write in your journal." Rachel smiled. "Be sure to write about your *wunderbaar* sister."

Judith raised her eyebrows. "What makes you think I still write in a journal?" She did still enjoy writing her thoughts in a journal, but ever since Peter moved out and married Ella, she hadn't shared a room with Rachel like they did when they were younger.

"You love to write. I figured you still take time to write in your journal. Although you might not have time now with seeing Jacob, studying for your GED and helping with housework." Rachel put the pins from her bun inside her *kapp* and stood.

Did Rachel think I'd quit helping with cleaning? "I'll always make time to help you with housework, even though it's my least favorite thing to do."

"I threw the housework in to see if you'd comment on it." Rachel looked surprised. "I thought cooking was your least favorite domestic thing."

"It seems like you like to tease a lot now that you're married." *I'm glad Rachel's lighthearted about a lot of things. Marriage has definitely been ideal for her.*

Rachel nodded. "Being married to Samuel makes me *froh*."

"I'm glad you and Samuel decided to live here. I'd miss our girl chats we have if you had moved when you married. You won't be far when you move into your new house but still it won't be the same. I'm in no hurry for you to move."

Rachel frowned. "I'm glad Samuel decided we should live here at first, but he's talking now about building in the spring. I hate to think about leaving here. I feel *gegisch* about being a grown married woman and wanting to live at my *daed's* home instead of my own home, but I can't help it. I've gotten so close to Noah and Matthew since *Mamm's* been gone. If *Daed* doesn't remarry this year, that's another reason for us to wait to move."

"Amish married couples live in their parents' homes all the time before they get their own places." Judith swung her legs off the bed and her bare feet touched the floor. She gave Rachel a hug. "Whenever you do move, we'll be sure to continue our sister chats. I want us always to be close."

Rachel hugged her back. "We'll be just like *Mamm* and *Aenti* Carrie except we won't have miles separating us. I'll see you in the morning. *Gut nacht.*"

After Rachel left her bedroom, Judith thought, *I hope Rachel's right in assuming I'll always be close in distance, and I don't plan on leaving Fields Corner. But I can't rule anything out. I want to experience many English things and what if I like them enough to want to leave Fields Corner? I'm glad I'm not getting baptized this year. I definitely need more time before making a final commitment for my faith. Or what if I develop strong feelings for Jacob? I can't see him leaving his family to live elsewhere.*

Chapter Nine

On Saturday evening Jacob sat in a booth across from Judith. Their new cell phones were on the table in front of them. "I wish you wouldn't have paid me for yours. It was my idea to get the phones."

"Why should you pay for mine? I won't be just using it to talk to you but also to Eliza when I have questions. It's an investment in my future. I'm going to tell *Daed* I have it. It'll be better for him to know I paid for it. Then he should realize I'm serious about getting my GED."

Jacob chuckled. "I think he knows how serious you are."

She grinned. "That's true. *Danki* for getting the phones. I'm a bit *naerfich* about using one, though."

"We'll practice this evening when we're both in our own homes. Maybe we should text sometimes. That won't use up as much money on our phones." He'd only bought a twenty-five dollar card for each phone.

"I'm not ready to text, but I do want to save our minutes."

"When we start texting, we can text the time we're available to talk to each other."

"I like that so we don't disturb our families with our conversations. I don't want to use the phone in front of my family. If we text the time, we can sometimes use our phone shanties instead to save our minutes. Or in your case, the barn. I remember Samuel said your phone's in your barn."

"Maybe when the weather's warmer, we can do that." *What was the point of freezing in the shanty or barn when we can be in our bedrooms to talk to each other?* Jacob thought.

The waitress brought their large pizza and order of cheesy breadsticks. Then she slid the spatula under a slice of pizza and put it on a small plate for Jacob. Then she did a second piece and put it in front of Judith. The young woman asked Jacob, "Is there anything else I can get for you?"

"No, thank you." Jacob glanced at the pizza. "It looks delicious."

"Okay, I'll be back later to see if you need any refills for your drinks." The waitress smiled at Jacob for a moment. "I remember seeing you here with the guys from the lumberyard. Do you work there?"

He nodded. "I do work there. I came here once for lunch. Our boss treated us because we got a big order done on time."

"You have a nice boss. I'll leave you two to enjoy your food."

Judith raised her eyebrows at him after the woman left.

"What's wrong?" The pizza with the pepperoni and mushrooms looked fine to him. It was what they ordered.

A faint smile curved her lips. "I'm surprised you didn't notice how the waitress was interested in you. And I'm sitting right here."

"I think she was just making conversation and being friendly. She wants a good tip is all." He took a sip of his Pepsi. "When Rachel waits on me at the bakery, she talks a lot and asks me questions."

Judith laughed. "Rachel's your sister-in-law. That's a big difference. Plus you were only here once with the guys but Claire remembered you."

"You're observant. I didn't even know her name was Claire. I bet you're an excellent teacher...always aware of your students' needs."

"Diverting me by complimenting me. I like it." Judith dipped a breadstick in the marinara sauce. "By the way, Claire has a name badge on her shirt."

After they ate quietly for a few moments, Jacob asked, "Have you had time to study for your test?"

"I've started studying the easiest subjects for me. I'm going to tackle science last. It'll be the hardest for me since we didn't have science in school. I'm worried about passing the science part."

He nodded. "It'll be rough. Apparently the bishops and other leaders don't think we need science to be successful on our farms or in our businesses."

"Which is fine if you become Amish." She took another piece of pizza and put it on her plate. "The pizza is yummy. My *bruders* told me to bring some home to them. I shouldn't have told them where we were going."

"I can get a pizza for them."

She shook her head. "They don't need it."

"Talking about *bruders*, Samuel's not happy about me getting my driver's license for work. But Katie is. She said I could be her driver for her catering business. But I told her I'm not buying a car. It's just for work and to make more money." Samuel said more than that to him, but he wasn't about to share all that with Judith now. One night he had shared a couple of beers with his friends and Samuel had found out. It was harmless and he wasn't going to make a habit of drinking alcohol. He respected the Amish's views about not drinking, but he was in his *rumspringa*. This was his running around time to try new things. He didn't want to have any regrets later that he'd missed trying something that wouldn't be allowed later when he became Amish.

After she swallowed a bite of pizza, Judith said, "It sounds like you've definitely decided to get your license."

"I started memorizing the driving rules. I want to take the written part this month."

She wiped her mouth with a napkin and said, "If you were English, you'd probably already have your driver's license. Have you ever thought how restrictive our lives are as children? English children dream of becoming doctors, veterinarians, firemen, astronauts, nurses, or maybe movie stars. My cousin Violet teased Rachel about becoming a movie star."

"You and Rachel both are beautiful enough to be movie stars. You look very pretty in your lavender dress." He noticed Judith's cheeks turning pink at his compliment.

"*Danki*, but becoming a movie star would never happen. Not that I want to be a star but you see my point. When you were a little boy, you planned on becoming a farmer, furniture maker, or maybe you did think about working in a factory or at the lumberyard." She sighed. "Women only think about growing up and getting married. Before doing that, we expect we'll teach, work in a bakery or make quilts for money— but not much else. If an Amish girl wants to become a doctor or a nurse, she'd be at a disadvantage right away. We have no science in our schools because it's been decided there's no need for us to learn science."

A flash of uneasiness went through his mind about buying the cell phones. Even though he was the one suggesting they should have them and he was also doing something else non-Amish by getting his driver's license, he felt grounded about his life. He wanted to join the church in a couple of years. But he worried about a cell phone being a bad thing for Judith. *I hope it's not the first step for her finding more freedom in the non-Amish world and leaving us.* "You left out buggy makers. I'm sure I can think of more careers that we consider. I see your point, but how many little boys actually become firemen or doctors after dreaming about these careers? Few, I'm sure."

"I think dreaming is an important part of growing up," Judith insisted. "We're robbed of having this special dreaming in our childhood by being raised in an Amish home. *Mamm* and *Daed* never asked me what I wanted to be when I grew up."

Claire stopped by their table with two more glasses of Pepsi.

Right now, I think I could drink a beer instead of a Pepsi. Judith's making me nervous. She's definitely not happy about our Plain way of life. It's obvious she thinks that the English have better childhoods. "Okay, what did you want to be when you were little?"

"A nurse. When I was eight years old, I was in the hospital for double pneumonia. I liked one nurse especially who took care of me. I even remember her name was Tara. I told my *mamm* that I wanted to be a nurse like Tara." Judith took a sip of her pop. "She told me Amish women didn't become nurses."

"Would you like to be a nurse instead of a teacher?"

She shook her head. "Not any longer. My *daed* told me that my mother was like a nurse with all the things she did while taking care of her *kinner*. I miss her a lot."

He reached across the table and grasped her hand for a moment. "I'm sorry. She was a *wunderbaar* woman. My mother misses her too. We all do." He gave her a little smile. "I hope she'd be happy that we're spending time together."

"I'm sure she would be. What does your mother think of you courting me?"

"She's *froh*. Of course, you know she and your mother both wanted Samuel and Rachel to be together, but *Mamm* didn't match us up before because I'm a few months younger than you. She didn't think I was mature enough for you...the beautiful and studious writer for *The Budget* and teacher for our Amish school."

Judith frowned. "I don't believe that. You're mature and have a *gut* job. But I guess sometimes girls grow up faster than boys."

"Katie definitely feels this way now. She doesn't think Tim's as mature as she is." He shrugged. "She's right because Tim told her how he wanted to marry her, and then he broke Katie's heart when he changed his mind."

"I hope Katie meets someone."

"I think she will eventually when the time is right." Jacob took a drink of his Pepsi. "Maybe I'll get my GED. We could study together."

Laughing hard, she quickly covered her mouth. After a few seconds, Judith moved her hand away from her mouth. "I thought I was going to choke on my pizza. I know you don't want your GED. You just want an excuse to spend time together."

"I'm serious. I'm afraid I won't be good enough for you if I don't have my high school diploma."

"How about I get mine first? Then if you still want to get yours, I'll help you study for it. Right now, I think you should concentrate on getting your driver's license." She fingered her *kapp's* tie.

Jacob looked at the empty pizza pan. "Since we don't have any pizza left to take to Matthew and Noah, how about we go to United Dairy Farmer's and buy ice cream to take to your home."

"That's a *wunderbaar* suggestion. The boys love ice cream."

When her blue eyes brightened, Jacob was happy he suggested getting ice cream. *I like Judith a lot and definitely want to continue seeing her.*

* * *

"*Danki*, Jacob, for buying ice cream. And not just any kind but chocolate chip cookie dough. I love this flavor." Rachel said. "And very thoughtful of you to buy cones so we didn't have to dirty bowls."

"You're welcome." When they were looking at the flavors of ice cream at UDF, Jacob had decided to buy a box of waffle cones for eating their ice cream instead of using dishes. He didn't want to make extra work for the women. Or for himself. Heck, he helped his *mamm* with dishes sometimes. Maybe some Amish men didn't do any household duties, but with Katie busy now with her catering business and his *mamm* looking tired after working all day at the bakery, he felt glad to help a little with dishes. During the winter months his *daed* pitched in occasionally to help in the kitchen even though he still had work to do on the farm—in the winter he wasn't nearly as busy as he was during the big spring planting.

Noah swallowed a mouthful of the ice cream. "*Ya, danki* for the ice cream."

"Jacob, keep courting Judith." Matthew licked his lips. "Are you taking her to Pizza Hut next Saturday?"

"That's rude, Matthew." Judith frowned at her brother. "And no, we aren't going to Pizza Hut."

"We plan on going to the Sunday youth singing." *Maybe buying a half gallon of ice cream to bring here was a mistake,* Jacob thought. *Everyone might stay up later with us. But I did get invited in by buying a treat, and it's nice sitting in the living room with everyone.*

"How's work at the lumberyard?" David asked.

"It's going *gut*. I like working there and I'm thankful for my job." Judith's *daed* seemed pleased with his answer.

"I'm going to head upstairs. I'm tired. It's been a busy week." Rachel stood. "*Gut nacht*."

"I'll be up soon," Samuel said while looking at Rachel.

After she left the room and they heard Rachel's footsteps on the stairs, Samuel turned to Jacob. "Has Katie mentioned hiring someone else to help her? I think it's too much for Rachel to work for Katie and *Mamm*."

Jacob grinned. "Especially now that she's married to you."

"I'm sorry I wasn't here this evening to do the dishes." Judith leaned forward in her chair. "I should have told her to leave them for me to do when I got home."

I hope Judith's not really sorry she wasn't home to do the supper dishes, Jacob thought. "Katie hasn't said anything about hiring anyone else to help her." Turning his head from Samuel to look at Judith, he decided to tease her. "I guess when we go out next, we can stay here until you do the dishes. Of course, I'll help you."

Judith grinned at him. "Okay, you're on. I'll cook on Saturday evening and you can clean up everything. I have to warn you that I'm a messy cook and I also use lots of pans."

"Oh no," Noah mumbled. "You better eat before you come."

Judith jabbed Noah lightly on his side. "I heard that. I'm sure I can cook something edible."

"*Ya*, you don't want to kill your boyfriend," Matthew said.

Judith chuckled. "You see what I have to put up with here."

* * *

Blackie and Jacob hurried home after leaving the Hershberger family. At the kitchen door, he only hugged Judith and told her he'd call her at ten o'clock. He needed to allow time to get home and to take the harness off Blackie. More than anything he wanted to kiss her but thought it was too soon to show this sign of affection.

When he was finally in his bedroom, Jacob called Judith. He'd already put her new cell phone number into his. When she answered right away, he was relieved.

"*Danki* again for getting our phones," Judith said in a breathless voice. "I enjoyed this evening."

"Me too. You're a fun and interesting person."

"I liked how you listened to me talk about my feelings about our Amish world. It was nice to bounce ideas off you," Judith said.

On his way home, he thought of something to mention to Judith about the whole daydreaming thing. "You can always talk with me about anything. I did think of something that's good about being raised Amish. An English guy I work with bought his sons GI Joe action figures and play guns for Christmas. He said how his boys want to fight for our country and join the Army when they grow up. Amish little boys don't mention going to war or joining the military. That's a *gut* thing."

"He might have said it because he resents the Amish's non-resistance stand against violence when others protect our rights by fighting," Judith said. "But you're right, I like how Amish children only see guns being used for hunting. Solving problems with guns is un-Christian. We learn at an early age to turn the other cheek like Jesus said to his disciples."

"He talks about his sons a lot so I don't think there was a hidden meaning meant for me. He knows I pay federal and state income taxes...like he does. I won't fight for our country, but I'm helping to pay for the military by working and paying taxes."

"That's true," Judith agreed. "I was just thinking that maybe we could study together sometime. I can quiz you on your driving rules— but probably it'll be better to study at your house."

"We can do that. Maybe at the bakery. We can enjoy coffee and dessert while we study."

"I like that."

He heard Judith sigh so asked her, "What is it?"

"I just remembered I didn't tell you that Eliza did know about my *Onkel* Scott being a senator. She learned about him when she heard about my grandparents dying in the buggy accident. She's not planning on writing anything about my famous *onkel*, but it is how she decided to use our school for her college classes. I'm going to do as much as possible without her help. I trust Eliza but I still don't want her to have to drive so far to our house."

He just thought of something that might work for Judith while she studied for her test. "The other day when I was getting coffee at the bakery, Rachel mentioned to me how Sarah Miller has her GED. Maybe she could help you study."

"Jacob, that's a great idea," Judith said in an excited voice. "I can light two candles with one flame having Sarah come to my house."

"I hope you don't mean now you can eliminate me as a study partner."

"I don't want to do that. I'm hoping *Daed* will like Sarah being at our house again."

After chatting for a few minutes, they decided it was time to get off their new phones so they wouldn't use up all the minutes too quickly. Jacob turned off his phone and put it in his top drawer of his dresser.

Before going to sleep, he gave thanks to God for his many blessings, but especially for his friendship with Judith. She was a beautiful and *wunderbaar* woman...one he could see spending his life with...as long as she decided to become Amish by joining their church.

As he climbed into bed, he thought, *I hope Judith doesn't decide to continue her education after she gets her high school diploma. If she does, I'm afraid I'll lose her to the non-Amish world, and she'll decide to go to college. But I want what's best for Judith. If she can only be content by attending college, I won't discourage her. I want her to be happy.*

Chapter Ten

On Wednesday evening, Rachel spooned cake batter into the cupcake holders. "I never should've told you about my new carrot cake recipe for cupcakes. It definitely takes more time."

Katie covered the huge pan of macaroni salad before putting it in the refrigerator. "I'm sorry. I shouldn't have put it on the list of choices for desserts. You look tired."

"I'm proud of you doing so well with your catering business in such a short time, but I don't know if I can keep this up with baking for you." Rachel opened the oven door and slid the cupcakes into the preheated oven.

"I know *Mamm* won't want you to quit working here." Katie leaned against a countertop in the Weaver's Bakery. "I only cater to one small business next week so I can do it myself."

"Won't you need me to help serve, though?"

"I'll get Mary to help. It'd be hard for you to serve because it's a breakfast meeting." Katie gave her a concerned look.

"*Ya.* Mornings haven't been good for me." Rachel suspected she could be pregnant with the morning sickness and tiredness she was experiencing.

Katie straightened and grinned at her. "Oh my gosh, you're pregnant. I'm going to be an *aenti.*"

Rachel shrugged. "I only missed one period. If I miss this month's, I'll buy a pregnancy test kit."

"You should get one now." Katie stared at her. "You don't seem *froh.* I guess because you and Samuel haven't been married long."

After she sat on a chair, Rachel said, "I want to have a *boppli.* I know it's a blessing if I am pregnant, but poor Ella has been wanting to get pregnant for two years. Samuel and I were just married. I know it'll be hard for her to hear my news."

"It'll be hard for Ella to hear you're having a baby already, but I think there's more to it than you being worried about your sister-in-law's reaction." Katie rested her hand on Rachel's shoulder. "I'm your best friend. You can tell me what's wrong."

"It'll be another reason for Samuel to say he should start building our house this spring." Rachel sighed. "I don't want to move yet. I like taking care of everyone in my family."

Katie grinned and took a seat next to her. "Or is it you don't want to live in a house with just my *bruder*? He can be a boring person."

Rachel laughed. "Samuel isn't boring. I look forward to sharing our new home with Samuel...but not this year."

"Do you wish you had waited to get married?"

Rachel shook her head. "I love being married. Even though, our property's a short distance away, it won't be the same. And *Daed* needs me to cook and clean."

"Judith can do more."

"She's been cleaning the kitchen and doing the dishes each night. She's going to cook one evening for us because Jacob's coming to dinner on Saturday."

Katie smiled. "So Judith's experimenting on you first. I remember how Noah and Matthew stopped in here after school while you were in Florida. They wanted to get something to eat before they went home to eat Judith's cooking. Those two were so funny."

"They already complained about Judith cooking this week. I'm sure she'll become a better cook. She just never has been as interested in it, but she's definitely better at quilting and sewing than I am."

"Jacob said the brownies she took to the ice skating party were delicious. I told him you probably made them. Did you?"

"Judith made the brownies. *Aenti* Carrie gave her the recipe. I should make them for one of your catering events. They're easy to make." Rachel exhaled a deep breath. "Oh, Katie, I think I am pregnant. I feel sick sometimes in the morning and I'm tired all the time."

"I'm sorry you aren't feeling well but if you are pregnant, it'll all be worth it. You're going to make such a *wunderbaar* mother." Katie patted her arm. "And Samuel's such a perfectionist that he'll take his time building your house."

"Samuel's hoping I'm pregnant. I'm glad the bakery's closed. I wouldn't want to talk about being pregnant in front of Mary. The whole town of Fields Corner would know I might be expecting." *I better tell Katie not to say anything to her mamm. I want to keep it quiet until I'm positive I'm pregnant.* "Don't tell your *mamm*."

Katie made a gesture that showed her zipping her lips and throwing away the key. "I won't say a word."

"I feel like I could fall asleep now...I'm so tired. Maybe I'm not expecting and it's because you're working me too hard."

Tucking a strand of brown hair under her prayer covering, Katie said, "I'll suffer and hire nosy Mary to help me when you get too big. Two single old maids should work okay together."

Rachel laughed. "Stop it. I was kidding. And you aren't an old maid. I usually don't mind working after the bakery closes. Samuel's a sweetheart about bringing me in the evenings to work with you. It's convenient that his store is next door, so he can work on his orders. I'm glad we can use your *mamm's* kitchen to prepare everything for your catering jobs. And it's romantic to be cuddled next to him in the buggy. Samuel and I enjoy the trips to town."

Katie was quiet so Rachel nudged her. "A penny for your thoughts."

"I'm afraid I was thinking how I could be pregnant right now if Tim and I had gotten married. I never would've started this business if he hadn't changed his mind about marrying me. I still miss him."

Rachel hated seeing Katie looking sad. How could Tim hurt Katie and start seeing an English woman? It was still hard for her to believe because she thought Katie and Tim made a *wunderbaar* couple. "Judith said you didn't go ice skating. I know it must be hard but you need to go to some social activities with other young adults."

"Jacob mentioned Luke King isn't seeing anyone. Jacob said that he saw Luke watching me after church service last Sunday. But why would he be interested in me? Tim rejected me. I don't know if I can take another man's rejection. I don't think it'll happen but what if Luke should ask me to go out with him, then decide I'm not what he wants in a wife? It'll be awful to be rejected twice." Katie smoothed her apron before raising her head to look back at Rachel. "You know, the women will have something to say at quilting."

"Are you kidding? Of course, Luke is interested in you and don't you dare put yourself down...you're beautiful, smart and funny. A little bossy at times, but otherwise you're perfect."

"Bossy, huh." Katie's blue eyes looked amused for a moment. "Maybe I'll go sometime to a youth get-together, and see if Jacob's right about Luke. I'm not going to get my hopes up. Who knows...Jacob is so smitten with Judith, he might be imagining Luke looking at me with interest."

"I'm sure Jacob's not imagining it." Rachel pointed her finger at Katie. "And no maybe. If you promise to go to the *next* youth get-together, I'll write an article about your catering business and how *wunderbaar* it is. I'll submit it to *The Budget* and English newspapers." She saw Katie's eyebrows shoot up about the article. "I can tell you don't have any confidence in my writing ability. I'll have you know that Samuel thinks I'm good with words. But I'll ask Judith to proofread the article after I write it."

Katie rolled her eyes at Rachel. "And I'm the bossy one."

* * *

Later on Wednesday night, Samuel pulled Rachel next to him in bed. "This is my favorite part of the day when you're in my arms every night."

"Me too. I love being married to you." She loved how her body molded to his in such a perfect fit. Cuddling with her husband gave her a lot of enjoyment. "Plus it's nice to have a warm body in bed on a cold winter night."

Samuel laughed. "I love having a practical wife."

"Katie guessed I might be pregnant. I told her not to tell anyone yet."

"I'm glad she realizes you might be expecting a *boppli*. Katie needs to give you time off to rest." He cleared his throat. "You know it's going to seem a bit different for your *Aenti* Carrie to buy things for the baby before she and your *onkel* buy a stove for our new house."

Oh no, he's going to talk about building our house. "I don't think it'll matter to *Aenti* Carrie."

"How about instead of starting in the spring, I wait until the end of the summer to start building? It'll still take me months to finish the inside. I plan on doing most of the work myself except I'll have Peter and Jacob help with what I can't do alone. Once we move, we can have Matthew and Noah stay overnight on the weekends. Just something to think about."

"I suppose *Daed* will visit us a lot in our home. He'll want to see his *grandkind*. He loves babies." *If Samuel starts building in the summer and takes his time, we won't move until a year from now or later.* "I don't want to move during the winter months but next spring sounds like a better plan."

"Your *dat* will want to see you too. He's a *wunderbaar dat* and will be a loving *grossdaddi*."

Why wait to get the pregnancy test kit? "Instead of waiting to confirm my pregnancy, I'll buy a testing kit tomorrow. If it shows I am, I don't want to tell Peter and Ella right away."

"We can wait to tell them except I'd like to tell my parents. My *mamm* would never forgive me if I don't tell her right away."

"*Ya*, I want to tell your parents and my *daed* as soon as we know for sure. I'll tell *Daed* not to say anything to Peter." Talking about her *daed* becoming a *grossdaddi* reminded her how Baby Weaver wouldn't know her *mamm*. Suddenly, an unhappy heaviness pressed on her heart. Samuel seemed to sense her sadness. He held her tighter and kissed her forehead. She ran her finger along his cheek and across his chin. "I love you with a beard. I didn't think I would."

"That's *gut* because I can't go without it. It's nice for people to know I'm taken and married. It stops women from flirting with me."

"At least, it stopped Mary Zook." Rachel giggled. "But I don't think you need a beard to show people you're married. I heard you tell your customers all the time how you're married to the best baker in your *mamm's* store and how everyone should be so fortunate."

"Mrs. Weaver, there's only one problem being married to you."

She loved hearing him say Mrs. Weaver. "What's that?"

"You talk a lot."

Before she could say another word, he gently pressed his lips against hers, sending warmth throughout her body.

* * *

Judith couldn't sleep because of what her *daed* said to her earlier in the evening. He told her visiting *Aenti* Carrie might be a *gut* thing to do. "Since you're determined to get your GED, then I'd rather Carrie help you study for it instead of that English woman, Eliza. Carrie got her diploma before she married Scott. I remember she passed it the first time. I'm sure you can do the same with her help."

"But *Daed* she took the GED test years ago. I can call *Aenti* Carrie sometimes instead of Eliza, but I don't think going to Kentucky for help is going to save me study time."

"Sure, use your new cell phone more to chat," he said sarcastically. "I don't like you having your own phone. I'm not happy with Jacob for buying it."

"*Daed*, I told you I gave Jacob the money for it and for the phone card. He didn't just go buy it without talking with me first. As I said before, we didn't get phone contracts. Having a cell phone is a temporary thing for me." She hated to think what he'd say when Jacob got his driver's license. What if he forbade her to see Jacob?

"I can understand why Bishop Amos allows some Amish business owners to have cell phones instead of landline phones in their stores, but you having one seems wrong."

"*Daed*, remember I'm in my *rumspringa*. I'm not baptized. It's okay for me to have a phone now. I promise I won't use it in front of the twins. Or in front of Bishop Amos."

"I wonder what Martha and Robert think of Jacob having a phone. I bet they disapprove too."

"Jacob hasn't mentioned their reaction." *If they had complained, I doubt Jacob would tell me,* Judith thought.

She loved *Aenti* Carrie, but she didn't want to spend time riding the bus to Louisville. Or paying a driver would be expensive. Hours spent traveling could be better used studying at home and going over the practice tests Eliza had given her. *Why is Daed so mistrustful of Eliza?* "Eliza and I are similar in a lot of ways...good ways. She lives at home while going to college. She has a job at Children's Hospital in Cincinnati and she plans on becoming a teacher. Her faith is important to her just like ours is."

"What is her faith?" David asked.

"She's Catholic and goes to church each week with her mother."

David nodded in agreement. "I understand she's a nice young woman, and I wouldn't mind your friendship with her if she wasn't so close to your age."

"*Mamm* was good friends with Sharon Maddox." She grinned. "And *Mamm* stayed Amish."

He gave her a small smile. "The difference is Eliza is a college student. I'm afraid if you spend too much with her, she'll convince you to go to college. Telling you to visit Carrie is my way of showing my support for you to get your GED, but going to college with Eliza isn't acceptable to me."

His support for her getting her diploma was a huge step in their father-daughter relationship. Seeing her *daed* looking tired and sad made her want to find a solution...she didn't want him worrying about her leaving their faith. *At least, not at this time. I can't rule out college completely.* Remembering what Jacob had suggested about Sarah helping her might be a *gut* idea to tell her father. She thought about asking Sarah first, but maybe asking her *daed* for permission might be better. It'd be embarrassing to ask Sarah, only to upset *Daed*. "Jacob made a suggestion you might like. I told him how Sarah Miller got her GED before she became baptized. He said she could help me study. She's closer and it hasn't been as long since she took the test."

David's expression of displeasure changed to relief. "I like that. Jacob's smart to court you and to suggest Sarah."

Before leaving the living room for bed, she hugged him and said, "*Danki, Daed.* I love you. I'll talk to Sarah after school tomorrow. *Gut nacht.*"

All kinds of thoughts ran through her mind while she tried to sleep. What would Sarah say? Would she be interested in helping her study? She didn't like making her *daed* unhappy. She wished he could understand how getting her GED didn't mean she would leave their Plain community. Eliza wasn't a bad person. Maybe the cell phone made him think Eliza was a negative influence. *I can't believe he'd rather I'd make a road trip to Kentucky to see Aenti Carrie.* Also *Daed* wasn't happy with Jacob for getting the cell phones but that wasn't a surprise. When she told him how Jacob suggested Sarah as a resource person for her GED study, her *daed* seemed relieved.

Being an Amish father must be difficult with the many outside influences. Poor *Daed* had to parent without her sweet *mamm.* And he still had Matthew and Noah to raise.

Ya, I'll go see Sarah tomorrow. I need to pass the GED test soon...for my own benefit and to cause Daed less stress. I feel like a hypocrite, though. I'd like to be able to spend time with Eliza and learn more about her college classes. I believe her that she won't include anything about Onkel Scott and Aenti Carrie. She punched her pillow and hoped sleep would come soon.

Chapter Eleven

Judith sipped her coffee at a table by the window in Weaver's Bakery. When Jacob asked her yesterday if she would like to meet him for an early dinner before they went home from their jobs, she was surprised. He liked to get home right after work to help his father with chores. But his *daed* told him he'd milk the cows. Rachel offered to take Matthew and Noah home. That was a nice thing about living in one household. When she wasn't available to take their *bruders* home, Rachel or Samuel were. Well, they could walk home by themselves, but it was nice in the winter for Matthew and Noah to get a ride in the buggy. *I'm glad Jacob's not here yet. It gives me a few minutes to collect my thoughts. I can't believe how gut life is.* God's blessings for her were overwhelming. She mentally started making a list of all the *wunderbaar* things in her life recently. *1) I obviously have a boyfriend now. 2) Daed hasn't kicked me out of the house. Of course, she knew he wouldn't do that, but I wonder if he considered it for a second. 3) Eliza gave me the push I needed to get my GED. 4) I can use the computer in the fabric store to do my online application. I can't believe they have Internet. I guess it helps that Sarah's business partner isn't Amish. 5) I'll be an aenti. So exciting about Rachel's pregnancy. No wonder she's been tired lately.*

"Geez, Judith, daydream much?"

She turned her head away from the window to see Mary Zook standing next to the table. "I'm sorry, Mary. What did you ask me?"

"Did you want to order anything while you're waiting? Maybe a piece of pie to go with your cup of coffee?"

Judith shook her head. "*Danki* but I'll wait for Jacob. I'm early. He should be here soon. We'll going to eat an early dinner."

"It must be nice to have a boyfriend, and one willing to spend money on you. Most Amish men are frugal and only take their girlfriends home after the Sunday singings. They don't want to spend money for special dinners at a restaurant."

"I don't know much about the dating practices, but I think you're right." *I'm glad Jacob is willing to be different from most Amish young men. I hate seeing Mary's sad face.* Fortunately, she remembered Jacob was going to see if John would be interested in Mary. Talking about this possible man for Mary might cheer her up. Jacob was such a thoughtful man, she thought. "What about John from the lumberyard? Have you had a chance to talk with him?"

Mary smiled. "He's nice but quiet. I'm hoping he'll get over his shyness. I'm glad Jacob introduced us."

"I hope John asks you out soon." She noticed Jacob entered the store. He removed his winter coat and hat, putting both on the hooks by the front door. His *mamm* knew Amish men liked having a place to put either their straw hats in the warmer months and their winter felt hats during the colder seasons. He wore the usual clothes that Amish men wore...a dark blue shirt with black pants and suspenders. Jacob's good looks took her breath away. She still couldn't believe he liked her. She wasn't as pretty as Rachel.

"Hello, ladies. I heard John's name so I'm guessing you're speaking about the bashful John I work with. He wants to ask you out this week yet. I told him that you don't bite, Mary." While taking a seat across from her, Jacob said, "I told John if he waits too long, someone else is going to court you."

Mary laughed. "Putting a tad of pressure on him might work."

After Mary left to give them a few minutes to decide what they wanted to order, Jacob smiled. "I'm *froh* you could meet me after school. All day I looked forward to seeing you."

Judith's pleasure at Jacob's words made her feel dizzy with happiness. "I'm glad you suggested meeting here."

"*Daed* seemed happy I wasn't going home after work. *Mamm* decided to quit early and Katie's going to close here for her. She should be in the kitchen working now. I'm sure my parents like to have alone time."

"That's so sweet." Jacob's parents' marriage seemed a lot like the type of relationship her *daed* and *mamm* once had. They loved each other deeply and enjoyed spending time together, whether it was raising a family, going to church, or just something simple like working on a puzzle.

"Do you know what you want to eat? I'm starving."

"I'm going to order vegetable soup and a grilled cheese sandwich."

"That sounds *gut* except I'll get a ham sandwich with my soup."

"Oh no, I thought of something. Your parents might not have a long time with just the two of them. Rachel and Samuel are going to visit to tell them their news." She smiled at Jacob.

"It must be *wunderbaar* news with that big grin on your face."

She nodded. "It is. I'm going to be an *aenti* and you're going to be an *onkel*. Rachel found out today that she's expecting."

"Does your *daed* know yet? They might tell him first before they head over to my parents' house."

"He doesn't know. Rachel just took a pregnancy test." Out of the corner of her eye, she saw Mary approaching their table. "We better be quiet. I'm not sure Rachel wants Mary to know yet."

Jacob whispered, "Once Mary knows anything, it becomes common knowledge."

After Mary left with their food orders, Jacob said, "I'm going to take the written part for my driver's license next week. Mike's giving me a ride."

"I'm surprised. I didn't think you were ready to take the written part. I haven't helped you study." Although they talked about studying for their tests together, they never found the time for it to happen.

"I've been studying the little booklet Mike gave me. I have to take the test on a computer so I've been learning how to use one at work in Mike's office."

"I'm sure you'll pass the test."

"I hope so because Mike's going to start teaching me how to drive once I have my permit. I need to make enough money so I can buy land before it gets too high for me to afford."

She smoothed her apron, thinking Jacob getting his license might not be a *gut* idea. *What if he likes driving so well, he decides to buy a car? Maybe Jacob won't pass the driving part. It seems like it'd be hard to learn to drive a truck.*

He gave her a questioning look. "What's wrong?"

She shrugged. "I know you insisted before that you won't buy a car, but what if you like driving the truck so well that you decide you'd rather drive a car instead a buggy to get places faster?"

Jacob, reaching across the small table, took her hand in his. "I'm only doing this to get money to buy land. Then I can build a house for my future wife and family. Besides, I love spending time with you in my buggy. It's nice to have you cuddled next to me." He paused. "Anyhow, I don't think Blackie would like to be replaced by a metal contraption with no personality."

Laughing, she said, "That's reassuring."

"I'm taking over for Mary," Katie said as she stopped next to their table. She flipped the white cup on the table over and poured Jacob's cup of coffee. "Judith, I better warn you that my *bruders* like to tease. They can be ruthless."

"It's especially fun to kid bossy sisters." Jacob grinned at Katie.

Katie frowned. "You're the second person to call me bossy. But that's okay, I'm sure an older sister has to be bossy at times when we have younger siblings to mother."

"Mentioning *bruders* remind me of Noah and Matthew," Judith said. "They're going to Ruth's house to get her dog after they get their chores done at home. Ruth left school early this afternoon to visit her sister and new baby in Berlin."

"So you'll have her students tomorrow?" Katie asked, giving her an inquisitive glance.

Judith nodded. "It's only for one day and Ruth will be back on Monday. I told her to stay longer. Her parents are traveling with her there, but are going to stay for two weeks. I told her I'll be fine teaching by myself. Ruth and I put the classes together sometimes for reading, so I'll do that tomorrow. It's nice to see how the older children help the younger ones."

"What happened to Mary?" Jacob asked.

"She's on the phone taking an order for a birthday cake," Katie said. "I'll be back with your soup and sandwiches."

After Katie left quickly, Judith said to Jacob, "I took your suggestion and talked to Sarah today about helping me study for my GED. I told *Daed* you thought of me asking Sarah for help." She sighed. "I planned on getting my GED last summer, but I got busy sewing dresses for Rachel, Katie, and me for the wedding. Then I noticed *Daed* and the boys needed new clothes for the big event. I never found time to study."

He squeezed her hand. "I know you'll accomplish passing the test with flying colors and soon you'll have your diploma."

"*Danki* for believing in me." She grinned. "I definitely want to hurry get it now that there's a Weaver baby on the way. I might have baby care duties later this year."

Katie brought their food and said, "So you heard the news too? I'm looking forward to being an *aenti*. Enjoy and I'll be back to refill your coffee."

* * *

"*Danki* for driving by Ruth's place."

"I'm happy to. It's not far from your house." Jacob looked at Judith's worried face. "I'm guessing you're afraid the boys might get in trouble at Ruth's."

"*Ya*, I have this weird feeling that something isn't right. I hope I'm wrong but I remember them telling me this morning how I was lucky I got to go ice skating this winter."

"We better check. Knowing your *bruders*, they might get it into their heads to get on the pond."

"I told them the ice might not be frozen hard enough now. We've had several days of above freezing temperatures." In a frustrated tone she continued, "But they sometimes don't listen."

"Boys will be boys. I heard *Mamm* say this often while growing up when my *daed* was upset with Samuel and me."

Judith cleared her throat. "If you decide not to drive truck for Mike, you can stay with your parents and won't have to worry about saving enough money to buy land."

He turned his head to look at Judith. "I'm not sure my bride would like that. She might prefer her own house."

"I'm sure she wouldn't mind living with your family. Your parents would be easy to share a house with, and I think it's *wunderbaar* how Amish families remain close." She paused for a moment. "I was surprised Eliza lives at home, but her college tuition is expensive and Xavier University isn't far from her mother's house. She might have decided to stay home, too, because her father was ill for some time before he died."

"We're getting close to Ruth's." He was glad they'd go by the pond before getting to the barn. Knowing Matthew and Noah, Judith could be right to be worried. He remembered walking on a frozen pond once when he was about their age. He and his friends ran off it when they heard the ice making cracking sounds. *I'm glad it's not dark yet. But it will be soon.*

He heard a dog's sharp barking before seeing the pond, but he didn't want to alarm Judith that something could be wrong.

"Please help us. Please save us," a boy's voice screamed.

Judith put her hands on the sides of her mouth and yelled, "Matthew and Noah, we're coming to help you."

"Hurry, I can't get Noah," Matthew yelled back. "He's under the water."

While Jacob flicked the reins, he said in a persuasive voice, "Faster, Blackie. You were right, Judith. You better call 911. After I get them out of the water, they might need medical attention." He didn't want to alarm Judith that maybe he wouldn't be able to get them out of the water.

Grabbing her purse, she opened it quickly and removed her cell phone. She flipped it open and after a moment said, "It's ringing."

Jacob barely got Blackie stopped by the pond when they both quickly jumped out of the buggy.

Matthew disappeared under the water. *Please God, help me save them,* Jacob prayed. *I can't go out on the ice and get them. With my heavier weight, I'll plunge into the water. I need some way to get them out. If only I had something in the buggy that I could extend to them.* Not a single thing came to his mind.

"The dispatcher said help is on the way." Judith's blue eyes were filled with fear. "But I don't think we can wait on them. They must be drowning. We have to do something."

Matthew's head popped up and threw out his arm, managing to hold onto Noah. "Noah's leg was caught on something but I got him freed."

"I'm so happy to see your faces," Judith cried to her brothers.

Both boys managed to stay above the water while Jacob started moving toward them. Knowing the ice was thin, he tried to spread out his weight as much as possible as he inched out toward the boys. He grabbed Noah first and pulled him from the icy cold water. Although he heard a slight cracking noise, Jacob felt God was with him. "Noah, go to Judith. She's waiting to pull you ashore."

Next Jacob reached out to Matthew, but when he grabbed on, the combined weight cracked the ice and they fell in.

"Jacob, I'm sorry I weigh more than Noah."

"It's okay." As soon as he fell in the frigid water, Jacob couldn't breathe at all. The air was gone. He'd never been this frightened before in his life. He prayed silently, *Lord, Matthew and I are fading fast, help us hold up long enough to be rescued.*

Chapter Twelve

Terror gripped Judith as she wrapped shivering Noah in the buggy robe...it was quilted and insulated. "Let's get you warmed up." Hopefully, it would help lessen the effects from being in the freezing water. She worried about Noah experiencing hypothermia, and it was a big concern for the two remaining in the water. *Help hasn't arrived so it's up to me to get Jacob and Matthew out of the pond,* she realized with clarity. Jacob's ashen face had scared her. What if he couldn't hold on to Matthew much longer? Losing both would be too heartbreaking. Hearing the sirens too late for their mother must not happen again now. She needed to focus on saving both of them. "Noah, you watch for the life squad."

She ran back to the pond and stepped onto the ice. Walking cautiously, she felt relief at no cracking sounds as she continued on the ice. She was relieved to see Jacob's head above the water.

"Judith, get off the ice. It's too dangerous," Jacob said urgently.

"I weigh less. I'll get Matthew out, then you." *Please, God, help me with each step I take not to break the ice. Thanks and praise to You for giving Jacob the ability to pull Noah to safety.* With darkness descending upon them, she appreciated the light from the buggy lantern.

"I don't know if you can pull me out. I might be too heavy," Matthew said in a worried voice. "Make sure the paramedics take care of Noah. He'll say he's fine when he isn't."

Her heart raced at the realization that she could also fall into the water. Judith heard the wailing of a siren in the distance; silently she gave a quick thanks to God. Her voice, saturated with relief, cried out to Jacob and Matthew, "I hear the squad. It sounds close."

"Judith, get off the ice before you fall in," Jacob said. "Matthew, stay with me, the life squad will be here any moment."

She saw Jacob trying to keep her brother from slipping deeper into the water. At the sounds of both a fire truck and an ambulance, Judith turned her head in surprise as both vehicles stopped by the pond. Relief flooded her body when she saw a fireman in a flotation suit hop out of the truck. Quickly, he was next to her. She recognized the fireman as Jacob's boss, Mike. While the ice remained intact, she only heard a slight breaking noise from the extra weight. Gently, he pushed her toward the spot where Noah was on shore. "Judith, I'll get both of them out. You go join your other brother. They're going to take care of him in the ambulance."

"Mike, am I ever glad to see you," Jacob said.

"Geez, Jacob. Isn't it a little cold to take a swim? Or did you decide to go ice fishing? If you wanted a day off work, you just had to ask." Mike continued talking as he reached for Matthew.

After managing to safely get off the ice, Judith was happy to see Mike help Jacob out of the water, and another firefighter in a rescue suit take Matthew to the ambulance.

Knowing it was time to alert their family members, Judith called home and left a message on their answering machine. Next, she called Jacob's parents because they needed to know what had happened. As she left messages and her cell phone number, all the time wondering if the boys and Jacob would be taken to the hospital for observation. If so, she hoped Rachel and Samuel could come to Ruth's to get Jacob's horse and buggy. *I want to go to the hospital with them. Right now, I wish Rachel had a cell phone.*

* * *

Judith pulled back the covers and climbed into bed. She pulled the blankets to her chest with one hand while holding her cell phone to her ear. "I'm glad your hypothermia was mild."

"It's *gut* you told me to go to Ruth's place. Matthew and Noah are lucky to have such a wise *schweschder*."

"I should've tried to get them out instead of you. I might not have broken the ice and fell in. *Danki* for saving their lives. If you hadn't done what you did, I'm afraid they wouldn't have made it until the rescuers arrived." Remembering how great Mike was about everything, she continued. "Your boss is not only nice, but he's a great volunteer fireman. He wasted no time in getting you and Matthew out of the water and into the ambulance."

"He's *wunderbaar* about everything. That's another reason I thought about getting my driver's license, so I could help Mike out with his business."

She heard Jacob exhaled a deep breath. "Are you feeling okay?"

"After my dip in freezing water, I don't know if I want to drive truck for Mike. Sure, the extra money would help, but at what expense to my spiritual life? Judith, I felt God's presence when I heard the ice cracking. I realized everything was in His hands and I had to trust Him."

"I don't want you to get your driver's license but it's your decision."

"How are the boys since they got home?"

"Rachel is reading to them and they are safe in bed." She gave a little chuckle. "I'm hoping their dunking in ice cold water put some sense in them."

"I'm sorry if I'm keeping you up too late. I'm not tired now. I just keep thinking what if you hadn't told me to drive by the pond. I think it was the Holy Spirit guiding you."

"*Ya.* I think so too. The Holy Spirit gave me the nudge we needed. We were blessed tonight, and I'm glad everyone survived."

Jacob laughed. "I bet Samuel is hoping for a girl now."

"Or at least, not twin boys." With all the excitement, she hadn't told Jacob about her other news. "Eliza mailed me a nice letter and a copy of the interview she did for her class. She also included what she wrote about Amish education. I'm pleased with what she said. She wasn't critical of the way we teach without computers, and even mentioned how high our scholars score on the state tests each year."

"I'm glad you met Eliza. She obviously thinks highly of you. I've never had anyone interview me."

"You might be in the news on television this evening. If it aired, I'm sure your *mamm* will hear about it at the bakery tomorrow. And I should write how you saved my brothers' lives and put it in *The Budget*."

"No, that's okay. I don't want any recognition. What happened today with your *bruders* made me think about having an emergency kit in the buggy. I want to be ready for any trouble they might get into."

"Did you and Samuel get into trouble when you were their age? I don't remember ever hearing about either of you upsetting your parents with any shenanigans." She wondered if maybe her brothers were worse because they didn't have a mother. They were to get Ruth's dog and go straight home, but they had to go on the ice instead.

"Samuel was always a *gut* role model for me. I smoked a cigarette once with a couple other boys. Fortunately, I hated it. Sometimes, it's..."

"It's what, Jacob?"

"It's hard being Amish when you're a man. When the guys at the lumberyard asked me to go with them on a few Fridays, I did and I drank beer with them."

She was surprised at this confession of Jacob's. "Do you plan on continuing drinking with them?"

"I better not because I like it too much. I can't stop at one beer."

"I'm glad you told me, Jacob." She realized that their relationship had taken another turn—one where they shared everything. Jacob shared what tempted him instead of keeping it a secret. But it was hard to hear because she never imagined Jacob would drink alcohol. Here, she'd been worried her *daed* wouldn't want her to date Jacob if he got his driver's license. *What would happen if Daed hears about Jacob drinking beer after work?* Her *daed* was totally against drinking. Apparently, his brother had a problem with alcoholism, and it was years before he went to Alcoholics Anonymous to get help. *Why couldn't Jacob be more like Samuel? No, she wouldn't want him to be like Samuel. She liked Jacob just the way he was...except for the drinking part.*

"It wasn't easy telling you but I thought you should know. I like you a lot, Judith."

"I feel the same way about you. I want us to be honest with each other. You mean a lot to me." She paused for a moment. "Have you ever gotten drunk?"

"No."

"I didn't even know there was any place in Fields Corner that served alcohol."

"Pizza Hut does but I'd never risk ordering any alcoholic drink there. Someone might see me. There's a small bar a mile from Fields Corner where the guys drink and play pool."

She didn't like the sound of a bar being close when Jacob obviously felt tempted to drink. "I know Bishop Amos serves red beet wine sometimes, but my father never even drinks wine. Have you prayed about this temptation, and asked for God's help so you won't go to the bar and drink?"

"No. But I'm going to. It's going to be hard to break the habit of going with the guys. Maybe I'll stop and see a certain pretty Amish teacher after work on Friday instead of going with the guys."

"*Ya*, I hope you do that."

"I'm looking forward to Saturday evening."

She decided to tease Jacob. "What's going on then?"

"You invited me to your house. I'm on the cleanup crew after you cook." He laughed. "Judith Hershberger, I know you remember. You aren't getting out of cooking. I'm sure it'll be delicious."

"You're the only one who thinks that. I overheard Noah tell Rachel to help with the cooking."

"I have every confidence in you."

"*Danki*. I appreciate a man with an optimistic attitude."

"So what's on the menu?"

"It's a surprise." She'd decided to fix chili because Rachel seldom cooked it, so there would no way anyone could make comparisons between the two of them.

"I like surprises. I'd better let you get some sleep. We both have to go to work tomorrow."

"*Ya*, we do. Oh, my *daed* told me that my cell phone was a blessing because I was able to call 911. But he said the cell phone is like the shanty phone and should only be used for emergencies." What if Jacob hadn't gotten the phones for them? Just maybe, God had planted the idea in Jacob's head. Some English things were definitely helpful, and as much as she understood the Amish reasoning against certain modern conveniences, she never would think it was a sin or a bad thing to have a cell phone. However, she agreed with limiting the usage of a phone. Maybe after *rumspringa* was over and she and Jacob joined the church, they could still have cell phones for such emergencies. A landline phone in a shanty or barn wouldn't have helped her brothers tonight.

"*Gut nacht*, Judith."

She murmured, "*Gut nacht*." After putting her phone in the drawer of her nightstand, she climbed out of bed and kneeled on the cold wood floor to pray again. She'd already given thanks for the rescuers arriving in time, but now she wanted to say a special prayer for Jacob. *"Dear Lord, Please give Jacob the strength to stop drinking beer with the men from work. I'm thankful he could share his interest in alcohol with me. Help both Jacob and me to always put You first in our lives. I give thanks for Jacob, Matthew and Noah surviving their ordeal this evening. Danki I had a cell phone for this emergency so I could hurry call 911. And a special prayer for Rachel and*

Samuel's new baby to be healthy. Danki for all your wunderbaar blessings. Glory and praise to You. Amen."

As she climbed back into bed and pulled the covers up to her chin, it was disheartening to think about Jacob drinking beer, but her heart felt lighter after praying for him. It was like it said in the Psalms that "God is the strength of my heart."

Closing her eyes, she thought about how trouble and trials were part of the world. *Although Jacob has a problem now, I know that can change. Prayer is a great gift God has given us. We can pray our way through any difficulty. I'll continue to pray for Jacob each day. I have faith in him being able to stop drinking. God will give Jacob the strength he needs.*

A soft knock on the door interrupted her thoughts.

"Judith, are you awake?"

"Yes, come in."

"Sorry to bother you but it took longer to read to the boys tonight." Rachel sat on the edge of her bed. "I'm thankful you and Jacob went to the pond."

"It was scary seeing Noah and Matthew in the icy water. I'm relieved they're okay now."

"With all the excitement, I forgot to tell you that Aunt Carrie is coming here tomorrow."

Judith sat up in bed, worried that she was the reason her *aenti* was visiting. "She must be coming to help me with the GED, but I wasn't expecting her. I thought she knew I'm going to Sarah's fabric store to register."

"No, it's something else. *Daed* actually called her back after he heard her message on the answering machine.

She's pretty upset that Uncle Scott's thinking seriously about running for president."

"I can imagine she's unhappy. She adapted to being a senator's wife but First Lady of the United States...that's scary. She'll be surrounded by Secret Service men. Or women. I think I read they now have a woman in the Secret Service."

Rachel shook her head. "You amaze me sometimes. You always know a lot without us having a television. Or do you have a hidden TV in here?"

She laughed. "I happen to read a lot."

"Maybe it's good you'll be teaching tomorrow when she arrives. Don't mention the Secret Service to her or anything associated with the presidency."

"I won't. Well, at least you know Samuel won't be interested in politics. I wonder if *Aenti* Carrie would've married Uncle Scott if she'd known he'd do this."

"I guess we never know for sure what changes are in store for us." Rachel twisted a *kapp* tie around her finger. "I'm glad I don't work tomorrow. She was such a comfort to me when I spent time with her and tried to sort everything out in my life."

"It's something when you think about the people we fall in love with."

"I knew it." A broad smile crossed Rachel's face. "You're definitely interested in Jacob."

"I am. I wouldn't have offered to cook for him if I wasn't. You didn't think I was just doing it for you, did you?" Judith teased.

"I suppose you're thinking about the type of man Jacob is because he risked his life to save Matthew and Noah."

Judith nodded. "That definitely was *wunderbaar*. When I asked him to drive by Ruth's, he didn't hesitate. But, I'm been also thinking how Jacob's the only man to ask me to go with him to a youth get-together."

"I see what you're getting at. I was only courted by Samuel. And *Aenti* Carrie only dated Uncle Scott."

Judith leaned closer to Rachel. "Do you think *Mamm* ever was in love with anyone else?"

Rachel shrugged. "I can't imagine her seeing anyone before *Daed*, but I suppose it's possible."

"I still can't believe Jacob likes me."

"I told you he was looking at you way before he asked you out. I'm glad he finally did." Rachel stood. "I'll leave you now so you can dream about Jacob."

Judith grinned. "And you'd better scoot or your husband will come looking for his little wife."

Chapter Thirteen

I'm glad I'm not working at the bakery today. And I'm glad Daed's done with his morning chores and came in. He might be able to make Aunt Carrie feel better about everything, Rachel thought, the next morning. Tears had glimmered in *Aenti* Carrie's eyes and Rachel wanted to be supportive. *She helped me with my struggle about what to do with my life. But what can I say to ease her turmoil?*

"I can't be First Lady of the United States of America. Me, a simple woman only wanting to be a wife and mother. I never wanted to be on display all the time, especially not in politics." Wrapping her hands tightly around the coffee cup, Carrie's lower lip trembled. "I never thought Scott would let them talk him into considering becoming president."

"Maybe he'll change his mind," Rachel said. "He loves to help our country. Could you encourage him to find something else to do, so he won't be in the public eye as much?"

Carrie sipped her coffee. "I wish. He told the committee to go ahead and there's already this huge groundswell. He loves challenges so he can't say no. I know he'd make a good president but that doesn't mean I'll be happy about it."

David looked thoughtful before speaking. "Does he realize how unhappy you are?"

"I told him I don't think I can campaign for him if he runs for president, and I don't want to give speeches. I'm terrible at it."

"But you're good at giving speeches," David said.

Carrie raised her eyebrows and managed a small smile. "How do you know? You've never heard me speak."

"That's true," David answered. "But Scott told me the audiences like your sincerity and you're a good speaker."

Carrie took a tissue out of her black purse and gently blew her nose. "I have a group of friends who now pray for me before I give a speech so that's helped, but we're talking about a national audience if Scott gets the party nomination."

"I guess I could drive up in my buggy when you speak," David said, looking at Carrie. "That might cause a distraction."

Rachel grinned at her father. "Security wouldn't let you close enough to take the attention away from *aenti*."

"Everyone knows the Amish are non-violent so the campaign people would be more worried about the horse making a mess." Carrie gave a small laugh. "*Danki*, though."

"I won't vote for Scott, and I'll tell our friends and relatives not to vote for him if he decides to run for president." David said in a wry tone of voice.

"*Daed*, you and other Amish seldom vote." Rachel remembered him only voting a couple times in local elections when it involved zoning issues. "I don't think the few Amish votes will help or hurt Scott."

"Actually, a large number of Amish attended a rally in Kentucky. Scott was pleased to see them. I've noticed those Amish who vote are many times younger businessmen with an interest in community affairs." Carrie glanced down at her jeans. "Well, what do you think about my disguise? I thought of wearing Plain clothing but thought that might look strange driving my car, especially since I had to stop and get gas."

"I've never seen you in jeans or pants." Rachel noticed her *aenti's* blonde hair wasn't in her usual neat chignon but touching her shoulders. She wore little makeup if any. "You look too young to be Adam and Violet's *mamm*."

"I only wear jeans in the house sometimes." Carrie glanced around the kitchen. "It's nice to be here. I've missed all of you."

"I'm glad you decided to make the trip." David reached across the kitchen table and patted Carrie's arm.

"Last summer Scott mentioned quitting politics because of the corruptness in the system. He said how people become dishonest after they're in politics too long." Carrie turned her head to look at Rachel. "And he hated how the media made it sound like you and Nick were a romantic couple when you weren't. He said the media puts a spin on everything to sell newspapers and magazines. He even mentioned then how if he ever ran for president, the reporters would camp outside our door...and yours, too, because of my Amish upbringing."

"What does Violet think about her *daed* running for the presidency?" Her cousin might be happy about it, because last summer she'd enjoyed working for her father.

"She's excited and mentioned campaigning for him. Adam said he'd campaign, too, but he hoped his help wouldn't be needed." Carrie sighed. "Even if Scott doesn't run in the next presidential election, I'm afraid he'll be asked about it in the future. I never knew I'd be a political wife when I married Scott."

"Would you like another roll and more *kaffi*?" Rachel asked her *aenti*.

Carrie shook her head. "No, *danki*. The cinnamon roll was delicious. The kitchen's filled with the wonderful smell of your freshly baked pastries."

"Irene told me how Joshua Glick wanted to court you. I think a lot of Scott, but instead of giving speeches, you could be slopping pigs," David said, deadpan.

Carrie giggled. "David Hershberger, you're a terrible tease. And I happen to know Joshua's bald now. At least Scott still has his hair."

Rachel was glad her father made *Aenti* Carrie laugh. What would happen if her uncle actually was elected president? she wondered. *It's hard to imagine we'd have close relatives in the White House.*

* * *

"*Danki* for letting me crash here," Carrie said, glancing at all of them sitting around the kitchen table on Saturday evening. "I love being with all of you."

Judith smiled. "I'm glad you decided to visit. And I appreciate you helping me study last night. It's relief I'm now registered to take the GED test." When she'd gone to the Fabric & Quilting Friends store to register on their computer, Sarah wasn't there. The other co-owner was busy with customers so she had to leave the store without registering.

"I'm surprised I remembered to bring my iPad. I left in such a hurry. At least I accomplished something on my visit." Carrie put her spoon into her bowl of chili. "Having chili on a cold winter's evening was a good choice. It's delicious, Judith."

Jacob nodded. "It is. The grilled cheese sandwiches are good too."

Matthew put more oyster crackers on top of his chili. "I love this. *Ya*, why didn't you cook like this for us when Rachel was in Florida?"

"I think Jacob inspired her to be a better cook," Noah said.

David frowned at his sons. "Judith did a good job cooking and taking care of us while Rachel was away."

Jacob, sitting next to Matthew, ruffled his hair. "Not only is Judith a *gut* cook, but she was smart to tell me to drive by Ruth's pond."

"I admit I haven't given cooking my best effort. I enjoy many other things more, but I realized recently that my lack of concentration has been the problem. When I really focus just on cooking, I don't burn anything." Judith grinned. "But Matthew and Noah, you might not want to try dessert. I think I'll just serve the adults my creation."

Samuel took a bite of his sandwich. "I know what Judith made and I can't wait to eat it."

"If I help clean the school each day for a week, could I have your dessert?" Noah asked.

"I was teasing. Of course, I'll give you both dessert." *What a nice switch to have my family wanting to eat a dessert I made,* Judith thought. *I'm glad I made the cheesecake cupcakes. They were easy to make but should look like I put a lot of effort into making them.* She smiled at Noah. "But I like your suggestion to help clean the school."

"Are you still looking for land?" Samuel asked, looking across the table at Jacob.

"Maybe, if the price is right."

"Seth Graber came to the store yesterday and said he's selling his farm," Samuel said. "His wife wants to move to Michigan where their children and grandchildren live now."

"Why am I just hearing this?" Rachel said, turning to look at Samuel. "That's perfect. If Jacob buys Graber's farm, he'll be close to our land."

This isn't good, Judith thought. *Jacob might decide to get his driver's license so he can make more money driving Mike's delivery truck. Should I mention Jacob doesn't need land? I better keep quiet because I shouldn't be expressing what Jacob needs to do about his future. It's not like we're planning on getting married.*

"So when are you two going to start building your own house?" Carrie asked. "I imagine with a baby on the way, you're anxious to get settled in your new place. Don't forget Scott and I want to buy you a stove."

Samuel shrugged. "Rachel's afraid to live with just me. I guess I'm pretty dull."

Rachel looked perturbed at Samuel's remarks. "Stop it. You know I'm looking forward to you building our house but—"

"Rachel's afraid to move because of us," Noah said. "It's okay you don't have to stay here forever. Samuel said we can visit a lot."

"Whenever you start building, I'll help you," Jacob said.

"*Danki*. Rachel and I talked about me starting doing the framing this summer."

David raised his eyebrows. "With the *boppli* due the end of summer, you might want to start earlier and get it under roof in the spring. I can help as long as I'm not in the fields working. I'm sure your *dat* and Peter will want to help." He grinned at Samuel. "Although I'm not in any hurry to lose your help with the morning milking."

"I can hammer nails," Matthew said. "I'm *gut* at building birdhouses."

Judith noticed Rachel's unhappy expression and knew the problem: Rachel wasn't ready to move to her own house. "When you do move, you'll be close by. You might get tired of us because we'll be at your house so often."

"We'll see. I haven't seen the midwife yet." Rachel fingered her *kapp's* white tie. "Isn't it great news about Ella and Peter expecting a little one? I couldn't believe it when Ella and Peter told us yesterday they're expecting a baby in July. She's already three months pregnant. We'll get to enjoy their *boppli* before the next one arrives."

Matthew quickly said, "You can practice taking care of their baby before you have yours."

Rachel rolled her green eyes at Matthew. "*Bruder*, I helped *mamm* a lot with you two when you were just newborns. Oh, maybe that's the problem. I dropped you and Noah on your heads so that could be why you don't have any sense at times."

Both boys gave indignant glances at Rachel before Noah said, "I hope that's not true. I think babies have soft heads."

"I'm kidding," Rachel said. "I never dropped either one of you."

David chuckled. "Rachel, I think you got your *mamm's* sense of humor."

"If anyone wants another bowl of chili, I'll get it for you." Judith stood. She was pleased that Samuel, her *daed*, and Jacob already were eating their second bowls of chili. What a relief that they liked what she had prepared for the Saturday meal.

"I'm saving room for dessert," Carrie said. "I better go home soon before I gain too much weight."

"I wish *Onkel* Scott could've visited with you," Noah said. "I wanted to show him my artwork."

"If you have any extra pictures you've drawn, I'd like a couple so I can frame them." Carrie patted Noah's arm. "I'm proud of you. And Matthew, I love the birdhouse you made for my birthday. I have *wunderbaar* nieces and nephews."

As Judith gathered the bowls, spoons, and small plates they'd used for the sandwiches, Carrie turned toward her. "I'll do the dishes. You cooked and Rachel worked at the bakery today."

"I'll help," Jacob said.

David and Samuel stared hard at Jacob.

Samuel's eyebrows shot up. "Are you trying to make us look bad?"

Jacob shook his head. "I told Judith I'd do dishes if she cooked."

"I appreciate the help." Carrie stood, walking to the sink. "I'll wash and you may dry, Jacob. Maybe we can get done before Peter and Ella come for dessert."

"*Aenti* Carrie," Noah said in a clear voice, "after you're done with the dishes, I want to show you a picture I drew of *Mamm*."

"I definitely want to see it." Carrie gave David a searching glance.

Her *daed* was quiet for a moment. Judith knew it was because of the strictness of the Amish not wanting any picture taken of any person in their faith…including drawings of faces. She held her breath, wondering if he'd object.

With a serious expression on his face, David said, "I decided in this situation that the *Ordnung* rule against any graven image doesn't apply to Noah's drawing of his mother. It can't be considered the same thing as worshipping a graven image when she's no longer with us."

Rachel blinked away the tears that filled her eyes. "One aspect of my pregnancy makes me sad and that's knowing *Mamm* isn't here to share our joy in having a baby. She won't be here to hold my baby or Peter's."

David nodded. "She would've been delighted about Ella and you both expecting. She loved her children and looked forward to having *grandkinner*. One of her favorite Bible verses was that children are a heritage from the Lord."

"I love that verse from Psalms too," Carrie said.

"It's hard not to have *Mamm* here, but at least the *boppli* will still be blessed with a lot of other close relatives. Like *Aenti* Carrie *and Aenti* Judith." Judith squeezed Rachel's shoulder. "And I better get busy making baby quilts."

Chapter Fourteen

"Are you sure I didn't disrupt your Sunday plans?" Eliza asked Judith as they sat at the kitchen table. She'd invited herself and her mother to the Hershberger home when Judith had called to ask if she could submit her interview to *The Budget*. Judith told her if it weren't accepted there, she knew another place that might be interested in publishing it. Articles about friendships between the English and Amish were always popular.

Judith shook her head. "I was *froh* when you said you'd like to visit us today."

"It feels great to be here and to catch up on everything." Eliza sipped her hot chocolate. Should she mention how awkward she felt asking to make the trip to Fields Corner this afternoon? Her last visit in January hadn't ended well with Judith asking her if she knew about her famous uncle. Judith telling her she didn't need her help in studying for her GED had made her wish everything had been handled differently. *But if I'd told her upfront that I knew about Senator Robinson being her uncle, Judith might have been suspicious of me anyhow.*

"It's nice you brought your mom. I enjoyed meeting her." Judith smiled. "I'm glad *Aenti* Carrie is still here. I couldn't believe how quickly they started sharing their favorite recipes."

Eliza glanced toward the living room to make sure that her mother still was in there with Carrie Robinson. Both women chatted as if they were old friends while Judith's dad worked on a puzzle with Matthew and Noah. In a low voice, Eliza said, "She needed to get away and see something different. My brother is getting married soon. Mom's upset because his girlfriend is pregnant. Mom's happy to become a grandmother for the first time, but of course, would rather the wedding happened first, then the pregnancy. Austin is going to buy Tina an engagement ring soon."

"We've chatted a lot about education, but I don't think I ever mentioned we don't wear jewelry. When a man proposes in our Plain community, he doesn't give an engagement ring, but instead gives her a clock or a china set."

"A china set sounds lovely and practical." *But I'd rather have an engagement ring,* Eliza thought. "What did Samuel give Rachel when he proposed?"

"She got a china set. He went to Cincinnati and bought one with so many pieces that we teased Rachel that Samuel wanted a large family." Judith scooped a melted marshmallow off the top of her cocoa. "When's Austin's baby due?"

"That's the other thing. The due date is the end of July, but Tina wants a church wedding so they need to hurry make wedding plans." Eliza sighed. "You probably don't have pregnant brides in your community."

"Actually we do. It's not often but it does happen." Judith wiped her lips with a napkin. "I love the marshmallows after they melt."

"Your hot chocolate is delicious. I don't make mine from scratch. I'm lazy and just open a packet and pour it into a mug."

"I use packets at school. But one isn't enough for my chocolate taste so I actually use more than one."

"When an unmarried Amish woman becomes pregnant, is she and her boyfriend excommunicated then?" Eliza knew from her own research that once a baptized member committed a sin, they were excommunicated. They were welcomed back when they confessed in front of everyone and asked for forgiveness. *I wonder if this is true in Judith's church district?*

"They might be excommunicated for a few weeks. If both partners are baptized and church members, they do what your brother is doing. The Amish couples almost always marry, but will have fewer guests and shortened celebrations on their wedding day. Also to show more disgrace to the couple and to discourage premarital intercourse, the wedding might be on a different day of the week than what is usually customary."

"Mom thinks they should have a church wedding but just invite a few relatives and close friends. But Tina doesn't want a small wedding." Eliza rolled her eyes.

"Tina even suggested they wait and get married after the baby is born, so they can have a large wedding. This seems to be happening more and more in our world. A lot of emphasis is on having a perfect and expensive wedding day."

"Amish women don't have a lot of time before any wedding because the engagement is announced during a church service a few weeks ahead of the wedding date. We don't use caterers, which makes the food preparation a huge task. Weddings are held in the bride's home, so that's another reason I didn't have time to study and take my test to get my high school diploma last summer. I was busy sewing clothes for everyone, including the attendants...except Rachel made her own wedding dress. If *Mamm* had been alive, she would've wanted to sew it for Rachel."

"I read Amish brides don't wear white. What color did Rachel choose?"

"She chose green. If I ever get married, I'll choose either blue or purple."

Eliza noticed a dreamy look in Judith's blue eyes. *I bet she's thinking about her boyfriend Jacob.* "Okay, tell me about Jacob. Are you two getting serious?"

"We enjoy each other's company a lot. I have to admit it's nice to text and talk with him on our cell phones. I know we shouldn't get too dependent on using phones, but it's nice during our *rumspringa* to have them."

"It's a blessing you had a cell phone when Matthew and Noah were in the pond."

"*Ya*, it was." Judith continued, "I cooked for Jacob yesterday for the first time. Well, actually not just for him but for the whole family. I never made chili before but the men took second bowls. I made grilled cheese sandwiches without burning them...and cheesecake cupcakes for dessert."

"You'll have to give me your recipes, especially the cheesecake one. I love cheesecake."

Judith nodded. "I'll copy them for you before you leave. Also I used two types of cheeses for the sandwiches. The whole cooking thing has been a concern for me. I'm sure you remember my *bruders* telling you how I can't cook. I'm trying to become better in preparing meals for the family because it's important for an Amish woman to be able to cook well. But that's not the only reason I'm cooking a little more for the family."

Eliza leaned forward in her chair. "I bet I know why. You're going to start a recipe column in *The Budget*."

Judith giggled. "I don't think that will ever happen. I'm not qualified to write a recipe or a cooking column. I need to give Rachel a break from cooking sometimes. She's does a lot here plus works part-time in the bakery and works for Katie's catering business. She's been tired lately with all she does and being pregnant."

"I'm sure Rachel's thankful she has you for a sister. It's exciting you'll be an aunt twice this year." Judith had told her on the phone how Ella and Rachel were both expecting babies.

"Okay, enough about me. Tell me if you are dating anyone special."

Eliza frowned. "I wish there was someone special in my life but there isn't. I was serious about Brett and thought he was about me until he canceled a date with me. I decided to go to the movies with a girlfriend and I ran into him at the theatre. He was on a date with this gorgeous woman."

"I'm sorry. I'm sure it hurt a lot to realize he lied to you, but it's good you found out what kind of person he was when you did."

"I felt like leaving the movie, but my friend said we should stay. I thought about dumping my glass of pop on him."

Judith laughed. "That would have served him right, but I'm glad you didn't waste your drink on him."

Eliza grinned. "I was thirsty."

"You're pretty and smart. I'm sure you'll meet someone else."

"I won't have a date for Valentine's Day. Last year Brett gave me roses and took me to a romantic dinner. I loved him and imagined we'd get married someday." Eliza paused for a moment, thinking how Brett hurt her. She thought they were good together. "Do you and Jacob have any plans for Valentine's Day?"

"*Ya.*" A worried expression crossed Judith's face. "We're going to this new little restaurant, but—"

"But what? Going out to dinner sounds like fun."

"It's not common for Amish couples to have romantic dinners at restaurants, especially on Valentine's Day. Jacob and I heard a bit of gossip about us going to Pizza Hut on a Saturday night, so I have mixed emotions about it now. But Jacob said we aren't doing anything wrong. I thought maybe we should go to Weaver's Bakery again because that doesn't seem to be an issue for the gossipers since his *mamm* owns the bakery."

"I'm sorry but it sounds like they are jealous. I think it's sweet of Jacob to want to treat you to dinner, especially when it's not common in your world." Eliza, twisting a lock of hair around her finger, asked, "Do your students...I mean scholars exchange valentines?"

"They already made their Valentine boxes and they will make their own cards to distribute to each scholar in the school. We'll have punch and cookies in the afternoon."

"Hey, with teaching plus increasing your workload around here and seeing Jacob, have you been able to find enough time to study for your GED?"

"I have but I'm not ready to take the test yet. I used *Aenti* Carrie's iPad so I could get registered."

"I'm glad you got that out of the way," Eliza sat straighter in her chair, "because Ohio will have a new GED testing series next year and the cost of taking it will be much higher. It seems like whenever they change something, they have to increase the cost. It's good you're taking it this year when it's a lot cheaper."

"I'm hoping to take it early next month. If I don't pass it, I'll have to wait four months before I can do the retesting, so I want to be able to get it in before the new GED series."

Eliza reached across the table and patted Judith's arm. "You'll pass the first time. In the meantime, if you have any questions, give me a call. I can drive you to the testing center." She knew Judith couldn't very well drive her buggy that far to take her GED test.

"*Danki*, but I hate for you to make the long drive here, then back to Cincinnati. Maybe I could get a ride to the testing place, and you could bring me home."

"I don't mind picking you up. Just give me a call when you have the time of the test."

"Hopefully, March will be warmer so I can call you from the phone shanty. February has had record cold temperatures. I'm sorry I haven't been good about keeping in touch. My phone minutes are low so I need to buy additional ones. I'm glad I had minutes on it when the boys fell through the ice."

Eliza glanced at the doorway and said, "Matthew and Noah have been quiet this afternoon." Even when she went to the barn to see Minnie with them, they hadn't said a lot.

"They are quieter than usual. Do you suppose God gave me this strong desire to want to learn more so I'd meet you?" Judith asked. "I feel blessed with how things have worked out and we're friends."

"It's pretty cool how God brought us together, and we have fun chatting together." Eliza turned her face away from Judith when she noticed her mom and Carrie entering the kitchen.

"I'm glad you brought your mom with you, Eliza," Carrie said, smiling. "Brenda and I learned we have a lot in common. She loves to knit so I showed her the prayer shawl I'm working on now."

Brenda held a deep rose shawl in her hand and extended it for Eliza to see. "Isn't is a pretty color? Carrie told me how she knits each shawl for an ill person. She prays for this individual while she's knitting, so she or he will be covered in prayer when it's finished." Brenda turned her head to look at Carrie. "I'm impressed with how you started a prayer shawl ministry in your hospital."

Carrie shrugged. "It gives me something positive to do while my kids are in college and my husband isn't around."

Judith stood, picking up the empty mugs. "*Aenti* Carrie started by knitting a shawl for her close friend, Rose, who had to deal with chemotherapy."

Carrie looked sadly at the rose shawl. "I've been thinking about her a lot lately. I guess that's why I made this in a rose color. She never complained except to tell me she was cold all the time. I spent a lot of time in waiting rooms when I drove Rose to her appointments. To help the time to go faster, I started knitting her a shawl. I prayed for Rose as I knitted it, but I'm afraid she lost her battle to cancer. She was a remarkable lady."

Brenda said, "I'm sorry about your friend. I wish my husband would've had a prayer shawl before he died from cancer. This is a wonderful ministry."

After looking at the shawl, Eliza handed it back to Carrie. "I remember reading Christ Hospital has a prayer shawl ministry."

Brenda nodded at Eliza. "Now that you mention it, I think there was something in the *Enquirer* about it at

Christ Hospital, but I know they didn't have this ministry at your dad's hospital."

While the older women exchanged email addresses and phone numbers, Eliza stared at Carrie. *How pretty Carrie Robinson looks in her navy blue dress with her blonde hair in an elegant chignon. She looks even prettier than in her pictures. I remember Rachel saying their mamm was five years younger than her sister Carrie. I'm thinking my mom and Carrie are both around the same age. Mom aged after Dad died so she looks older, but Carrie must be around fifty too. It's interesting to have the famous senator's wife in the same room with me. News reports have said that Senator Robinson might run for president in the next election.*

* * *

Shortly after Eliza and Brenda left, *Aenti* Carrie also decided to leave. But first she planned to stop at Peter's house on her way back to Kentucky. Noah and Matthew went to the barn to feed Minnie, so it was only Judith in the kitchen with her *daed*.

When Judith heard a car in the driveway, she said, "I wonder if it's Ruth's with her driver." She mentioned stopping here to get her dog on Sunday. I thought she'd be here earlier, though. It's too bad Eliza and her mom already left."

David left his spot by the kitchen table and looked out the window. "You're smart. Always a step ahead of your old *daed*. How I got such an intelligent daughter is beyond me."

She laughed. "Stop it. You exaggerate. You have more wisdom than I'll ever have."

As soon as David opened the kitchen door, Ruth Yoder stepped inside and said, "Hello. I'm sorry to be running late. We had more snow up north around Berlin."

Judith grinned. "You should've used that for an excuse and stayed longer to help your sister."

"Now why didn't I think of that." Ruth put her small bag on the floor. "How did it go on Friday?"

"Your scholars were well-behaved." Judith stood. "Here, sit and I'll get you a cup of *kaffi*."

"*Danki*. A cup of *kaffi* sounds *wunderbaar*." Ruth removed her coat. "If you need to take a day off, I'll take your class for you. I loved seeing my new baby niece. She's so precious."

As David sat beside Ruth, he said, "It's too bad your sister moved away."

"*Ya*, it is. I told Miriam and her husband, Joseph, they could continue to live at my house. They considered it until Joseph's dad became ill. Also I only have a few acres. Joseph's main interest is in farming."

"It's too bad you didn't get to enjoy your little niece longer. Maybe you can go again soon." *I could suggest we get a substitute the next time,* Judith thought.

Ruth laughed. "I know how hard it is during the winter. The boys start getting into trouble when they don't get to run off some energy outside during recess."

David cleared his throat. "Actually two boys did get themselves into a predicament, but it wasn't during school."

Ruth's eyebrows shot up. "What happened? Was it Matthew and Noah?"

With a puzzled look on his face, David said, "How did you know it was my sons?"

"Believe me, it wasn't difficult. What did they do now?" Ruth tucked a stray lock of her light brown hair back under her *kapp*.

Judith began, "On Thursday evening I started thinking how the boys said I was lucky I got to go ice skating this winter, so I worried they might get on the pond when they got your dog. Even though I warned them not to, I had a feeling Jacob and I should stop and check on them."

"Oh no, don't tell me they went on the ice. The temperatures rose before I left. I'm guessing you got there in time to stop them from doing something foolish."

"They were both in the water, Ruth. While we were driving to your pond, we heard them yelling for help. I called 911, and before anyone came, Jacob managed to pull Noah out. But when he tried to get Matthew out, the ice cracked and Jacob fell in," Judith explained.

Ruth's eyes widened. "That's awful."

"Fortunately, Judith had a cell phone and could call for help, or instead we might have lost Matthew and Jacob," David pulled on his beard. "Judith started going on the ice herself to try to rescue Matthew and Jacob."

"I was so frightened Jacob and Matthew would drown before an emergency squad arrived. But then the volunteer firemen arrived and rescued both of them."

"I'm sorry. I should've known better and brought Buddy to your house. I told them after they got Buddy to go straight home. Did they have to go to the hospital for hypothermia?" Ruth spoke hurriedly. "If they did I'll pay their bills. It's the least I can do after all the trouble caused because I asked them to get Buddy."

"No, it's not your fault, Ruth," David said. "They didn't need to go to the hospital."

Clutching her purse, Ruth said, "I'll get Buddy and head home. Where are the boys?"

"They're in the barn playing with Buddy. I don't think they will get into trouble for several days. Falling into your pond might have knocked some sense into their heads." Judith grinned at Ruth. "So maybe a good scare was worth it and will eventually save them from making a future misjudgment."

"Stay and eat with us, Ruth. Samuel and Rachel went to Pizza Hut. They're bringing supper home for us." David studied Ruth for a moment. "I'll take you and Buddy home in my buggy. You don't have to walk. It's a cold night."

Judith couldn't open her mouth to insist Ruth stay to eat with them, because she was stunned to hear the eagerness in her *daed's* voice.

With a surprised look on her face, Ruth said, "*Danki*, David. I'll stay."

Noticing a pleased look on her *daed's* face made Judith wonder about the sudden interest he had in Ruth Yoder. While those two chatted, she felt ignored. *In a way, it makes sense, I guess. Ruth taught all of us but I thought if Daed ever remarried, a widow would be the best for him... like Sarah Miller. And Ruth is only thirty-five. I'm proba-*

bly getting way ahead here, they are just talking. It doesn't mean he wants to consider Ruth as a future wife.

But as she glanced at Ruth and her *dat*, she noticed they were both laughing together. *I guess Rachel and I aren't the greatest when it comes to matchmaking for our father. He definitely wasn't interested in Sarah Miller.*

Chapter Fifteen

"Let's hope we don't have a repeat of last Thursday with your *bruders* getting into trouble," Jacob said.

"I locked them in their bedroom so they can't misbehave. Unless they start a fire in their room. That's always a possibility." Judith saw Jacob's amused expression. "I can tell you don't believe me."

Jacob laughed. "For a brief second, I did. Are they still busy doing their extra chores?"

She nodded. "They have to do extra work for *Daed* for a month. They also have to pay some of the ambulance cost."

"I can pay some of it. I should've thought of that. They treated me, too, in the ambulance."

She shook her head. "No, you shouldn't pay any of it. My *bruders* are the reason you had hypothermia."

"Hey, you two, I see we had the same idea." Mike patted Jacob on the back. Mike was dressed in jeans and a navy blue sweater. "I'm sure the food won't be as good as

Weaver's Bakery, but my wife suggested we give the new restaurant some business for a change."

Jacob grinned at his boss. "I won't tell my *mamm* on you. She told me to check out her competition."

"How are your brothers?" Mike smiled at Judith.

"They haven't gotten into any trouble for a week, but Matthew did mention he'd like to be a fireman like you. You made quite an impression on both boys." When Matthew had talked about becoming a firefighter when he was an adult, her *daed* kept quiet. They both knew it'd be hard for Matthew to even volunteer as one when getting to the fire department quickly was essential. An Amish buggy ride would take too long.

"Hey, maybe they'd like to visit sometime and see the firehouse."

"I think that's a great suggestion," Judith said, wondering if she should ask if the whole school could visit. She decided not to ask, because it was something that needed to be discussed first with Ruth. "Thanks, Mike."

"Well, I better get back to my wife. Enjoy your dinner."

After Mike left, Jacob said, "I'm glad he didn't mention me learning to drive tonight, even though I know he's anxious for me to be a driver. He's afraid he'll be shorthanded this spring because a couple of guys are quitting. That's his main concern."

She didn't want to hear about Jacob driving. A couple of days ago he'd passed the written part and received his learning permit. She'd congratulated him but her heart hadn't been in it. But what could she say when he was understanding about her wanting to get her high school diploma? *I shouldn't be a hypocrite and tell him he shouldn't get his license when rumspringa is the special time for both of us to experience things in the English world. But what if Jacob changes his mind about joining the church after he gets his license? Having his own car might be next on his list of things to accomplish. He mentioned that he'd only drive Mike's truck, and he didn't have a desire to own a car. But the thrill of driving and getting places quicker might cause him to change his mind.*

She knew her *daed* now accepted her using a cell phone for emergencies, but he'd never accept Jacob driving a car instead of a buggy—or a truck, even though it would be for his job.

"You're quiet all of a sudden. What's wrong?" Jacob asked. "I think the chicken tenders are delicious."

"The chicken tenders are moist and good. I'm glad you suggested coming here. I'm sorry I was just thinking about our *rumspringa* and my *daed*. He's still unhappy about me getting my GED, but he never said a word when *Aenti* Carrie helped me register on her iPad. I'm wondering what he'll say about you driving an truck."

Jacob reached across the table and took her hand in his. "I understand. If getting my license and driving means your *daed* won't allow me to see you, then I won't do it. Samuel and my *daed* are against me driving too. Mike will have to hire other people. Sometimes I wish Mike had never asked me to get my license."

Even though he only held her hand for a brief moment, his touch made her insides feel warm. "*Danki*, Jacob. You're sensitive and sweet." She sighed. "Our way must seem silly to non-Amish. We can't always depend on our buggies and horses to get places, and have to hire drivers to take us when we have to travel farther. I know they must wonder why we can ride in their cars, but we can't drive vehicles ourselves."

"The important thing is we know why we can't and..." His voice trailing off, Jacob raised his eyebrows. "Leah Hostetler just walked in with her sister."

Turning her head slightly, she looked toward the restaurant's front door. She saw Leah's sister following the hostess to their seats, but Leah stopped walking to stare at Jacob. "Well, Leah noticed you."

"She must be visiting her sister. Leah moved with her parents to a farm in Indiana. They sold their farm here to Leah's sister and brother-in-law."

"I remember hearing that." Will Jacob mention that he dated Leah? Had he kept in touch with the pretty Leah? *I shouldn't worry about him wanting to see Leah again. He's definitely my boyfriend. He's always texting me or calling me on my cell phone. We've spent a lot of time together ever since we went ice skating. He has to be invested in our relationship, especially since most Amish boys are frugal, like Mary said. He's taken me out to eat—even during the week. From what Rachel said, Jacob had only spent a short time dating Leah before she moved.*

Just when she was convinced that she didn't need to worry about Leah being in the restaurant, her possible adversary stood next to Jacob.

"Jacob, it's *wunderbaar* to see you again." Leah was a small-boned woman, wearing a winter black bonnet and a black winter coat over a brown dress. Leah glanced at Judith and gave a quick nod. "I've missed living here. I might move back and live with my *schweschder*."

"How are your parents?" Jacob asked. "They might not want you to move and leave them. I remember how close you are to them."

Leah shrugged her shoulders. "They're well and Indiana is far to travel by buggy, but going in a car we're only two hours away. I couldn't see them daily, but we could have nice visits. I realize I was immature when we dated, I've grown up in the year I've been gone."

What was Leah implying? Was she letting Jacob know she was available and interested in him? I'm sitting right here, Judith thought. She felt like being rude and telling Leah to be quiet. She'd try an indirect but effective approach in letting Leah know Jacob was now her boyfriend. "Fields Corner has grown a bit since you left, and there have been other changes here. Remember, how I never attended the youth get-togethers, but Jacob invited me to one last month, and we had fun ice skating together at Ruth Yoder's pond. Last Thursday Jacob and I ate at his *mamm's* bakery. I was worried my *bruders* would do something foolish when they got Ruth Yoder's dog, so after we were finished eating, Jacob drove by her pond, and sure enough they were yelling for help. They decided to walk on the pond and with the higher temperatures, they fell through." She smiled at Jacob. "But praise God that Jacob immediately went on the ice and pulled out Noah."

"It was scary," Jacob said. "I fell in trying to save Matthew, but luckily Judith called 911. They came in time to rescue Matthew and me."

"You probably shouldn't have allowed those two near Ruth's pond." Leah gave her a hurried glance before turning back to stare at Jacob. "I'm glad you were around to help. You're a strong man, Jacob."

"Don't let us keep you. I think your sister is anxious for you to join her," Jacob said in a firm voice.

"We'll have to catch up sometime. You know where the farm is." Leah laughed. "We spent some fun times together."

"Leah, I hope you have a nice visit with your sister, but I won't be—"

"Good-bye. I better join my sister," Leah said as she interrupted Jacob and walked away from them.

"She left fast." Judith grinned at Jacob. "I guess she decided that your times together weren't so much fun."

"Leah must have me mixed up with someone else. We only went to a couple of youth sings. When Leah first moved, she wrote to me and I wrote her back. Then when she wrote me again, I wrote to her to have a *gut* life in Indiana. I even said that I hoped she met someone special."

Their server, a middle-aged woman, appeared by the table. "Did you save room for dessert?"

"I did." Jacob continued, "We'd like two hot fudge sundae cakes, please."

Judith shook her head. "I can't eat any dessert."

The server smiled at them. "How about I bring two spoons because it's a huge dessert?"

"I can eat a few bites." *What fun, sharing a dessert with Jacob on Valentine's Day. I can't believe I actually have a boyfriend,* Judith thought.

After enjoying her several bites—instead of a few— of the amazing chocolate cake topped with yummy ice cream, whipped cream and two cherries, she definitely felt full.

As they walked to Jacob's buggy, Judith said, "*Danki,* Jacob. Everything was delicious."

"I have something else for you."

"You already gave me a card and a box of candy. I don't need more." She was worried because she'd only given Jacob her homemade brownies with a little Valentine's card she'd bought at the discount store.

"I hope you will like it. I'll wait until we're in a more private spot." Jacob unhitched Blackie from the post by the restaurant.

A private spot...maybe he's going to kiss me. Did he ever kiss Leah? I hope not so he won't have anything to compare to. I've never kissed anyone except family members. She felt so nervous that she couldn't think straight.

When he opened the door of his buggy, he helped her get inside. "The temperature has really dropped. It's cold enough to use my battery heater." He reached behind the seat, his arm touching her shoulder as he did. Jacob put the heater close to her feet and turned it on.

"The warm air feels great. *Danki,* Jacob."

He flicked Blackie into action, and within minutes the buggy rolled down the road toward the outskirts of Fields Corner. When they reached a small town park, Jacob turned Blackie into a spot by a covered picnic shelter. He quickly put the reins down and said softly, "I can't wait any longer to give you this gift. He pulled her close and placed a light kiss on her lips. "I've wanted to kiss you for some time."

Her pulse raced at the feel of his lips on hers. Her first kiss...she was glad it was Jacob kissing her and hoped that meant they might someday get married. She was falling in love with him. "What took you so long? I've been wondering how long it would take you to kiss me. I heard Weaver men like to kiss."

He chuckled. "You surprise me sometimes, Judith. What else have you heard about Weaver men?"

"Not much but I'd love to learn more about a certain Weaver man."

"I think a second kiss should be a good education for you, Miss Hershberger."

His warm lips brushed hers, sending the pit of her stomach into a wild spin. When he suddenly broke the kiss, Jacob studied her under the park's light. "You're beautiful," he murmured.

"Beauty is vanity," Judith whispered.

"*Ya*, but I still say you're beautiful."

"I never thought that I was beautiful but *danki*. I've always thought of Rachel as being the pretty one in the family." Feeling uncomfortable talking about her looks, she quickly asked, "Did you learn more about the Graber's farm?"

"*Ya.* It's a good-sized farm...about seventy acres. I took a tour of their home. It's a nice two-story house. Mr. Graber is asking a fair price for it. But I don't have enough money to purchase it. I make good wages at Mike's lumberyard, but with the portion I give my parents, I don't have enough saved to buy it."

"I'm sure your parents would loan you what you don't have."

"I need to pray about what to do. Maybe God wants me to stay home and continue to help my *daed* farm. But I'd like to have my own place too." He grinned at her. "How about a kiss before we go back to your house?"

"I'd love another one of your sweet kisses."

Chapter Sixteen

As Jacob pulled his buggy into the barn, he was happy to see his father. He definitely needed to talk to him about what to do. Should he buy Graber's farm and go into debt? Or wait until he was older to buy a farm.

"How was work today?" Robert asked.

"*Gut.* It's Friday." He wouldn't mention that Mike gave him a short driving lesson. A snowfall was predicted for the area, so Mike wanted Jacob to get behind the wheel to gain some confidence while driving on a few dry back roads. Instead of taking one of the business trucks, Mike had him drive his personal, smaller truck.

Before they'd ventured outside the lumberyard, he'd driven for ten minutes on the lot, and then Mike had given him several rules of the road. But he couldn't talk to his *daed* about driving a truck. He was torn about the whole driving thing, and at times, wished Mike had never encouraged him to drive.

While unhitching Blackie, Jacob said, "The Graber farm is for sale and is about the size of your farm. I'm thinking of buying it but not sure it's the right thing to do."

"*Ya.* It's a nice farm. I can loan you some money for the Graber's land and house, but I think you should wait a few years to buy a farm. Or maybe not buy one at all." Robert pulled off his hat and ran his fingers through his thinning gray hair. "Your *mamm* and I talked about you having our farm when we get older. We can build a *Grossdaadi Haus* for us."

Jacob removed the harness from Blackie. "What if I don't join our church? Can I still stay here?"

Robert cocked his eyebrows at him. "I think you know the answer to that."

He smiled. "*Daed*, you know I like to tease sometimes. *Danki* for saying I can stay here. But I keep thinking I should be like Samuel and have my own farm for my wife."

Robert shook his head. "Fathers like to pass their farms on to their sons. Our farm is too large for Samuel since he has the furniture business in town. But I'm glad you want to farm. Choosing to be a farmer is making a commitment to a way of life which encourages family unity. Your children will learn to work along with you."

"While growing up I always liked working on the farm with you and Samuel."

"It can be hard to have two women under the same roof, but I think your *mamm* is easy to get along with. It might be too early to mention this, but she'd love to have Judith for a daughter-in-law."

Jacob chuckled. "I think what *Mamm* really wants are lots of *grandkinner*."

"*Ya*. You're probably right. You and Judith are still young so there's no rush. Once you marry, it's for life so you need to be sure to marry the woman God wants for you."

"I hope it's Judith." After Jacob brushed Blackie, he scooped out oats and put it in the horse's feed box. "She's going to get her GED soon. It's important to her."

"Usually, if any Plain person leaves the community to get their GED, they have plans to get a job in the English world or to get a college education. Why does Judith want a high school diploma?"

Jacob looked at his *dat*. "She loves to learn. I think if she hadn't been born in our world, she would've gone to college. But I hope getting her GED will be enough for her."

"Katie said Judith changed her mind about getting baptized with her and Rachel because of this whole education thing. I hope you're right about Judith. It'd be difficult for David to lose her to the English world. Hard for Rachel too." Robert looked closely at Jacob. "And hard for you."

He might as well get everything out in the open with his *daed*. "I'm surprised you haven't said anything about my *rumspringa*."

"It's your time to make a big decision about your commitment to our way of life," Robert said as he fingered his gray beard. "I don't want to interfere with the process of working through what you need to before you decide to get baptized."

"*Danki.*"

"You have a good head on your shoulders, but I'm not happy about you learning how to drive." His *daed* frowned. "It's your time to try out English things, but it seems to me you're only doing it to make more money. I don't think that's the way to do it. You make good money at the lumberyard without driving a truck for your boss."

"I'm not going to make money from woodworking like Samuel does. I'm not interested in making pieces of furniture. I definitely want to farm, but that's not a sure thing financially. Some years our crops are poor from bad weather conditions. When I can't make enough money from farming, I'll have to continue working at the lumberyard." Jacob exhaled a deep breath. "Maybe driving to make extra money to buy a farm isn't in God's plan for me."

"It's interesting that Judith thinks having her GED is important when she teaches in an Amish school where you only need an eighth grade education. And you're learning to drive a truck so you can make more money to buy a farm. You two seem to have a lot in common." Robert started walking away, but turned to give a backward glance at Jacob. "Katie's closing Weaver's Bakery this evening so I'm going inside to see your sweet *mamm*. Now, there's a woman I have a lot in common with."

As Jacob watched his *daed* leave the barn, he wondered, *What did he mean by saying Judith and I have a lot in common? Did he mean because we both are confused about what is right for us to do? Well, Judith seems definite about getting her GED, but I'm not sure about getting my driver's license. But I'm certain about wanting to farm. I just don't know if I want to buy Graber's land and house. On one hand, I'd like to be independent and have my own place, but staying here is a good option too. I need to pray about it.*

As he closed the door to the barn, Jacob thought how a lot of God's message to man was written in farming language in the Bible. According to Scripture, farming was a sacred lifestyle. He mentally repeated his father's favorite verse, 2 Corinthians 9:6: "Remember this: Whoever sows sparingly will also reap sparingly, and whoever sows generously will also reap generously."

Farming would be a *gut* life for him, his future wife and children.

* * *

After the dishes were done on Friday evening, Rachel whispered to Judith. "Follow me upstairs to my room. I need to talk with you about something."

Once inside Rachel's bedroom, Judith closed the door. "What's up?"

"*Daed* surprised me today when he told me he called Ruth from the phone shanty. Apparently, he told her he'd take her home after school because of the snow."

"I wondered why he showed up to take Ruth home. He knows I take her home when the snow accumulates.

That's why the boys and I went in with Samuel this morning. The snow was already falling hard."

"He said Samuel's buggy would be crowded with all of you, and he wanted to talk in private with Ruth about the boys." Rachel never remembered their *dat* talking to Ruth about any of them when they were scholars. They all had Miss Yoder for a teacher, but their *mamm* usually went to teacher-parent conferences to check on their behavior and progress in school. Of course, their *mamm* wasn't around to do it any longer.

"When the boys and I went to Samuel's store, we saw *Daed* and Ruth eating pie and drinking *kaffi* at the bakery. I don't think they were talking about Matthew and Noah. They were laughing and leaning close to each other."

"Do you think this means *Daed* is courting Ruth?" Rachel asked. "I mean, this isn't the first time he took her home. He drove her home after she ate pizza with us."

"Before you and Samuel came home that evening, *Daed* seemed eager to talk to Ruth. I felt ignored. I can't believe I forgot to tell you about how he acted, but I thought later maybe he was *froh* to have another adult closer to his age to talk to."

Rachel frowned. "But she's not close to *Daed's* age. She's in her thirties."

"She's only a little older than Sarah Miller, and we tried to fix them up." Judith sat on a chair and smoothed her apron.

"But that's different. Sarah is a widow. Ruth hasn't been married. I never thought about *Daed* being interested in a woman who's never been married. He'd have more in common with a widow. They'd be able to relate to each other."

Judith shrugged. "Maybe he doesn't want to court a widow. He could've courted the bishop's widowed sister, Barbara. He definitely wasn't interested in her. I thought Sarah being a Mennonite might have put him off."

"I don't blame Sarah for not having us over for supper." Rachel removed her *kapp* and removed the pins from her blonde hair. "It feels *wunderbaar* to have my hair down. I think Sarah knew we were trying to fix her up with our *daed*."

"She lives in an apartment above her fabric store. I think Sarah's considering moving back with her parents so they can rent the apartment. She might have decided her place was too small to invite us."

Rachel picked up her brush from her dresser. She brushed her hair, saying, "If I tell you something, you have to promise not to tell anyone."

Judith raised her eyebrows. "I won't tell on you. You know I can keep a secret. When you told me about *Aenti* Carrie giving you a picture of *Mamm* to keep, I never told anyone."

Rachel laughed. "You couldn't. She gave you one too. You didn't want to get into trouble for having a picture."

"I wonder if she ever gave a picture to *Daed*."

"I don't know. I can't believe you aren't dying to know what I did."

"I'm guessing you developed a new recipe, and you want to surprise everyone with it."

Rachel shook her head. "That wouldn't be much of a secret. When I spent time with Violet before I married Samuel, she took me to her hair salon. The beautician cut four inches off my hair."

"Why would you do that? We aren't supposed to get our hair cut."

"That's why I did it. I hadn't been baptized yet. It didn't hurt to get a few inches cut off. It helped to make my hair a little lighter. Let's face it, we have to keep our hair pulled back and tucked under our *kapp*. I have heavy hair."

"I can't believe I didn't notice, but you have lots of curl in your hair, so it's harder to tell."

"I won't do it again. I know it's wrong for me to do it now that I'm baptized, and to do so is against the *Ordnung*. But I'm mainly mentioning it to you because you should get a few inches cut off while you can. You know...before you get baptized."

"*Danki*. Maybe I will."

A *wunderbaar* idea struck Rachel. "You can have Eliza make an appointment for you. After you pass your GED, she can take you to a salon to get several inches cut off your hair."

"I'm glad you mentioned the GED. I think I'll go ahead and take it in March because if I fail any subject, I can retake just the failed subjects. After this year Ohio is going to make you take the whole GED exam again, even if you only fail one subject. Also next year it will only be available on computer. I want to take it on paper this year. It will be a lot cheaper."

Rachel remembered Judith said there were five subjects on the test. "Well, you should pass all of them. You're smart enough."

"I'm going to take their practice test so I can see what I need to study more."

At the sound of a knock on the door, Rachel jumped slightly.

From the other side of the door, David said, "I need to talk to Judith."

"Come in, *Daed*," Rachel said, wondering why their father wanted to talk to Judith. He seldom knocked on their bedroom doors. If he had anything to say, it was said to his children downstairs. When they were younger, he sometimes came to kiss them good night and to remind them to say their prayers. *Oh no,* she thought, *maybe he heard about Jacob learning to drive Mike's truck.*

"Ruth and I decided to get *kaffi* and pie after school at the bakery. While we were there, board member Gabe Fisher told me he heard you were going to get your high school diploma. He wondered if this could be true."

Judith's blue eyes widened. "What did you tell him?"

"I told Gabe you wanted to get your GED. I reminded him you were not baptized so this was the best time for you to pursue it. I didn't like telling him he was right. I don't want you to lose your teaching job." His eyes filled with doubt. "But do you want to stay and teach in an Amish school? Gabe asked me what your plans are after you receive your diploma."

"*Ya*, I love teaching at the Fields Corner Amish School. Nothing has changed." Judith gave a concerned look and said, "I know Ruth feels the same way you do, *Daed*. She wishes I'd forget about getting my diploma. Did she say anything about it to you?"

He nodded. "She thinks you'll need to decide soon if you're going to join the church. Bishop Amos mentioned to Ruth how it'd be *gut* for you to be baptized this year since you're a teacher in our Amish school."

"Ruth never said anything to me about Bishop Amos talking to her about this," Judith said with a frown.

I better get Daed off the subject of baptism and high school diplomas, Rachel thought. "What kind of pie did you have, *Daed*?"

A puzzled expression crossed David's face. "Apple pie. Why do you ask?"

"I wondered if you chose what I baked. And you did."

David smiled at Rachel. "Ruth ate a piece of your apple pie too. She said you make the best pies."

"Do you enjoy spending time with Ruth?" Judith asked.

He didn't answer immediately and had a thoughtful look on his face. "I do. Ruth Yoder is one interesting woman. Your *mamm* and I had stimulating conversations. One thing I've missed a lot is having a woman to talk to." Walking toward the doorway, David said over his shoulder, "*Gut nacht.*"

After he left the bedroom, Judith giggled. "What are we? Aren't we women?"

Chapter Seventeen

Cincinnati, Ohio

Closing her textbook, Eliza decided to take a break from studying for her exams. She was seldom bored because she had many interests—one was reading. Eliza thought how surprised she'd been to learn Judith had read *Pygmalion*. Her Amish friend said she loved to read as long as it was clean reading. Judith mentioned how reading was an integral part of her life as well as her family's. Fields Corner didn't have a library, but they checked books out from the bookmobile that came once a week. But at the moment Eliza didn't want to read. She needed to ask her mother what she thought about inviting Judith to their house.

It amazed Eliza how spending time with Judith at the Hershberger house had enriched her life. Her original perspective of Amish life changed drastically after learning more about their beliefs. Before she thought they were hypocritical in only driving buggies, yet the Plain people would ride in cars when the need arose to travel longer distances. By rejecting certain types of modern life and accepting others, it appeared to Eliza that the Amish contradicted themselves. But after talking with Judith and Rachel, she understood how owning cars would disrupt the slow pace of their Amish living. They didn't think that automobiles were evil, but owning them would make mobility much easier. Family members might spend extended periods away from home which would be bad. Also owning a car would cause inequality in their community because only proud individuals would show off their wealth by owning an expensive car.

As soon as her mom got off the phone, Eliza wanted to talk to her about Judith. Glancing at her mother, she smiled. Carrie Robinson and Brenda Dunbar talked almost daily or emailed each other. Who would have thought her mom would become friends with the popular senator's wife? Carrie trusted her mom and never seemed concerned that there was an ulterior motive behind Brenda's friendship.

She sighed. That hadn't been the case with Judith. Fortunately, Judith wasn't suspicious of her now. *But I can see why she thought I might be using her for my own gain. I was writing about her Amish life and asking a lot of personal questions. I hadn't been honest in the beginning and didn't mentioned I knew her uncle was Senator Robinson.* In the past, the Hershberger family had been targeted by the press. First, their grandparents died and the media appeared at the funeral. Later, a photographer sold pictures of Rachel when she was enjoying the beach with her famous relatives.

"Bye, Carrie." Brenda put the cordless phone down. "Carrie told me how she used to go to Fields Corner to help Irene and the girls to can. After Irene died she continued to help Rachel and Judith with the canning. She'd take a few jars home for her family. Did Judith ever tell you about what they call a *frolic*?"

She shook her head. "It sounds like a dance and I know Amish don't believe in dancing."

"Apparently, a *frolic* is a time for adult sisters to get together to visit with each other while doing chores such as canning food, cleaning house, shucking corn and more. They meet once a month and rotate houses and by helping each other out, they get their own work done, and have fun together while doing it. With living three hours away from Fields Corner, Carrie said she only went to help with canning, but the *frolic* was one of the things she always missed when she left the Plain community. Carrie mentioned how the Amish community comes together for everything. They provide care for members when they need help physically and financially."

"Judith didn't mention a *frolic* but she told me about their quilting parties. I'd like to sometime buy one of Judith's quilts. Her quilts are beautiful."

"I'd like to see her quilts." Brenda, picking up the coffeepot, asked, "Would you like coffee?"

She nodded. "Coffee sounds good. I need the caffeine so I can study more."

Brenda filled the pot with filtered water. After measuring the grounds, she pushed the button to start brewing the coffee. "Carrie puts out a small garden herself but doesn't have enough from it to can. She mentioned we should go this summer to help Judith and Rachel with canning their vegetables. Or I'll go, at least. I know how busy you are. I told her I'd like to help with their canning."

Eliza grinned. "You're getting so domestic on me. You talked last week about learning how to quilt and now canning. You aren't running a fever, are you?"

"I guess the Amish influence is rubbing off on me. But your great-grandmother did a lot of canning. She also made the most delicious strawberry jam." Brenda shrugged. "Sometimes I wish we didn't live in the city and we could have had more land. I loved living in the country when you were little, but it was a long commute for your father to drive to work. It made sense to move closer to his job."

"If we did have a bigger yard, I'd have a lot more to mow." After her father died, she had taken over mowing the small yard. "We both love Cincinnati. I wonder if we could rent a spot for a garden that would still be close enough for us to take care of it."

"That's a great idea." Brenda pushed a lock of her strawberry-blonde hair away from her face. "I love your new sweater. I wish we wore the same size so I could borrow it."

"I bet it'd fit you." Eliza glanced at her navy blue sweater. "You and Carrie sure talk a lot."

Brenda removed two mugs from the cabinet. "It's like we're kindred spirits. We both have absent husbands. Obviously, it's not the same because I lost my husband to cancer, but Carrie says she loses her husband daily to politics. Carrie said he's gone a lot and even when he returns home, he's occupied with doing the best job he can representing Kentucky."

"Mom, I'm glad you and Carrie are friends, but..."

"But what?"

"I'm here if you need to talk about anything." Eliza knew her mother was lonely a lot. Her parents had been close and theirs had been a solid marriage. What a blow it'd been when her father died from cancer.

"I know and I'm glad you decided to stay home this year. I enjoy spending time with you." After she poured the coffee, Brenda put the cup in front of Eliza.

"Thanks, Mom. You make the best coffee." While her mom sat next to her on one of the stools by their kitchen countertop, Eliza said, "I'd like to invite Judith here. I thought I could take her to the GED test and maybe to campus. I'd like her to see where I go to college."

"We can go out to eat after I get off work, or I can cook for you girls." Brenda sipped her coffee. "When does she plan on taking her test?"

"Around the middle of March which is perfect because I'll be on spring break. Judith went to a public library and took the practice test and saw what areas she needs to study." Eliza gave a soft laugh. "It's too bad she won't be tested on high German and Pennsylvania Dutch. Judith speaks three languages because the Amish use high German for spiritual occasions, like church services, weddings, funerals and Sunday morning songs; Pennsylvania Dutch is spoken at home and they use English in school."

"That's incredible that they speak three languages. I'm glad you decided to contact Miss Yoder and went to Fields Corner to learn more about the Amish and their teaching methods. I'm proud of you."

A warm spark of fulfillment settled in the middle of her chest. Although she was in college, it was still nice to receive her mom's approval.

* * *

Fields Corner, Ohio
Four weeks later...

Where was Jacob? Judith glanced again at the kitchen clock. Sure, he said he'd be late because of work, but it was now eight o'clock. Since they were in the month of March, it was understandable that the lumberyard had lots of building orders to fill. *But I could've gone with the rest of the family to Peter's for supper if I'd known he'd be this late.* She was anxious to tell him her big news. She didn't want to text him or call with what came in the mail today.

Hearing a crunch of horses' hooves hitting the gravel driveway, she went to the window. A rush of relief flooded her when she saw Jacob climb out of his buggy to hitch Blackie to the post. She opened the door before he knocked. "I was getting worried about you."

Jacob gave her a weak smile. "I'm sorry."

"Would you like *kaffi* or hot chocolate?"

"No, *danki*. I had *kaffi* before I left." He removed his coat and hat, putting both on the hooks by the door.

"I have so much to tell you. Let's go to the living room."

After they were seated next to each other on the only sofa in the room, she stared at Jacob. "Something's wrong. What is it?"

"I want to hear your news first," Jacob said in a firm tone.

She smiled. "I received my scores for my GED test. I passed with flying colors. I almost had a perfect overall score. I'm relieved I don't have to take it again, and I won't have to pay a driver another time to take me to the testing center." Eliza had seemed disappointed when Judith had hired an English driver to take her on a thirty-minute ride to Hillsboro to take her paper GED test. But, as she tried to explain to Eliza, she wanted to make all the arrangements herself. Besides, it wouldn't have make sense for Eliza to make the trip to pick her up and take her to a test center in Cincinnati.

"Congratulations, Judith. I'm not surprised." He squeezed her hand. "I knew you could do it. Like I've said before…you're the smartest and prettiest girl I know."

She laughed. "I didn't think you knew that many girls, so I'm not sure if I should take that as a compliment or not."

"So what's your next step? Are you going to leave Fields Corner to attend college?"

"I'm not going to college. You're stuck with me." At times she wasn't sure God was listening to her many prayers, so it was hard to know what she should do. But finally after more prayer time God had given her the assurance she needed. She now felt confident about her decision not to attend college.

He clasped her hand. "That's *gut*, but I thought you were impressed when you visited Xavier's college campus last week."

"I enjoyed seeing where Eliza takes her classes, and it's been nice learning more about college from her. I suppose if I'd been born in an English family, there's a chance I'd have attended college and liked it." She paused for a moment. "But I was born in in an Amish family."

"You sure you won't have any regrets if you don't go to college?"

"I won't have any regrets because I no longer want to go to college. I felt like I should have the freedom to choose, but I realize that I'm okay with where I am now. Even though an Amish person doesn't need a high school diploma, I think it was important I did get mine. Bishop Amos, the deacons, and the school board members...and Ruth see that I'm staying here to teach. I realize God has plans for me right here in Fields Corner. I'll continue to teach and to write for *The Budget*...and submit to other Amish publications. I might even see if I can write a column for an English newspaper." She grinned. "My love of reading will continue, because I'll still have my nose buried in books whenever possible."

"I'm happy for you."

Was Jacob being sincere? His voice didn't sound pleased. "Jacob, tell me what's bothering you."

"It can wait."

She frowned. "No, it can't wait. I care about you."

"I did work a little late, but I also went with the guys after work. I'm ashamed because I drank beer with them."

She didn't know what to say to him. He'd told her he couldn't stop at one beer so he wouldn't drink again. She'd been praying for him not to give in to temptation. "You drank more than one, didn't you? That's why you drank *kaffi* before coming here."

He nodded and exhaled a deep breath. "I know it was wrong and I don't want to make excuses for what I did."

"How often has it happened?" Although she hated to ask, she had to know if he'd been drinking on a regular basis.

"This was the first time since I mentioned it to you last month. I haven't gone with the men until this evening."

"Why did you go this time with them?"

"I guess I wanted to forget about my problems. I was feeling a lot of stress. I want to be independent, but I can't buy the Graber farm on my own. I don't want to drive the truck for Mike, but I haven't been able to tell him. He's been spending time teaching me to drive. I hate to disappoint him. *Daed* said now he'd loan me the money if I join the church. How can I take instructions and become baptized when I'm not worthy?"

The farm again. She knew how much he liked the Graber farm, but thought he had decided to continue to live at home. "The Amish are allowed to have personal problems. You're worthy. You recognize your issue with drinking and know it's wrong. This is our *rumspringa* so it's not like you joined the church, then started drinking."

"But what if I do join the church and continue to drink?"

What should I say? Please, dear heavenly Father, give me the right words to encourage Jacob, she prayed. "God will give you the strength you need to avoid this temptation. I believe in you, Jacob. When you were in the water, you felt God's presence. He loves you and will always be with you as long as you allow Him in your life." She squeezed his hand.

"You're right. I need to give my fears to God."

"I'm glad you feel free to talk to me about your drinking. I think it's God's will for us to help each other."

Jacob fingered a lock of her hair which had escaped her prayer covering. "You have beautiful blonde hair." After a moment of hesitation, he said, "I wanted to buy the farm for *us* but I can't."

His nearness and words caused her heart to beat faster. "I don't need the Graber farm. If we marry and it sounds like that's what you're inferring, I can live anywhere with you."

"Even in a chicken coop?" He grinned at her.

"As long as the chickens aren't in it." She laughed. "Gathering the eggs was a chore I loved giving to my *bruders*."

Pulling her to him, Jacob kissed her. "I love you, Judith."

He'd never told her he loved her before, but she had hoped he felt the same way she did. "I love you too." Judith rested her head on his strong, muscular shoulders. Although she didn't mind living with Jacob's parents, it was obvious he wanted to have his own place for them. "Instead of buying a farm the size of the Graber's farm, what about buying a smaller one? Maybe thirty acres like Samuel bought. It will be more economical for you to buy."

"I wonder if Seth would sell me half of his farm with the house. Or forty acres might be better for me. Seth could make more money by splitting it."

"That's a *wunderbaar* idea. I hope it works out but really don't get stressed out if it doesn't. God has a plan and maybe it's not the time for you to buy land." *Should I suggest we take instructions so we can join the church? Maybe it's better if I just mention what I plan on doing.* Lifting her head she stared at Jacob because she wanted to see his reaction to what she was going to say. "I want to talk to Bishop Amos about taking instructions this year. It's the right time for me to do this, so I can continue teaching in an Amish school. I've been praying about it, and I feel I'm ready to become Amish."

He frowned. "We'll have to give up our phone conversations and texting. I love being able to talk to you a lot when we don't see each other."

"With spring almost here, I can go to the phone shanty."

"We both better keep our cell phones in case your *bruders* need emergency help again."

"I think my *daed* would agree with us keeping them for emergencies when we can't get to a landline phone." She thought of another reason to keep her cell phone, but didn't think she should mention it to Jacob. Rachel had experienced several episodes of spotting and Ada, the midwife, had suggested that she should be seen by an obstetrician. If something serious happened with Rachel's pregnancy, a cell phone might be crucial to getting medical help.

"I need to tell Mike I'm not going to take anymore driving lessons from him. My parents will be relieved. And Samuel never liked it I was driving Mike's truck." Jacob kissed her forehead, then continued, "I'll talk to Bishop Amos soon and join the church this year. I promise I won't drink again. But I think we should still wait another year or two before we get married."

"I agree. I want to teach longer." She'd quit teaching after they married, but could always return as a substitute teacher when needed.

Sitting next to Jacob, she was happy to know this was where she belonged...not on a college campus but here next to her future husband. And her place was among her family too....her *daed*, Rachel, Peter, and the twins. God blessed her with a *wunderbaar* family, Jacob, friends, and scholars. He'd given her a special place on earth to live while serving Him.

Fields Corner was the only place she wanted to be, she thought as she cuddled next to Jacob.

About the Author

I grew up on a farm outside Findlay, Ohio, and I often acted out characters from my own stories in the backyard. In high school I would read during classes and hide a novel in front of me in a propped up textbook. After my high school graduation, I attended Ohio State University. Then I became a schoolteacher and play director.

I met my husband while teaching at an orphanage, and we married three years later. It took me that long to convince him I was the one for him! While raising our family in southwestern Ohio, I started writing nonfiction and was published. Later, I decided it would be a nice escape to write fiction. We were blessed with five daughters and one son. Two daughters were born with Down syndrome and live with us. Our other children also live close by in Ohio so that's wonderful. Our son and daughter-in-law have an adorable son and are expecting a little girl soon.

I've published through a variety of houses, including Samhain, Whimsical Publications, Desert Breeze Publishing, Publishing by Rebecca J. Vickery, Booklocker.com and Victory Tales Press. Around a year ago, I decided to self-publish my books, so I requested my rights back to my previously published stories. From the beginning, I've enjoyed self-publishing my Amish romances.

OTHER BOOKS BY DIANE CRAVER

Inspirational Romance

A Joyful Break, Dreams of Plain Daughters Series, Book One

No Greater Loss

Marrying Mallory

Romantic Suspense

A Fiery Secret

Contemporary Romance

Whitney in Charge

Never the Same

The Proposal – as a short and also in A Christmas Collection: Anthology

Yours or Mine – a novella

Historical Fiction and Inspirational

A Gift Forever

Visit Diane online!

Website:
dianecraver.com

Facebook:
facebook.com/#!/pages/Diane-Craver/153906208887

About the Book

After living in our Cape Cod house for twenty-five years, we decided to downsize to a smaller house. In 2013, building and moving took more time than I expected so that is my excuse for taking longer to publish *JUDITH'S PLACE*. I also have a seasonal job scoring the tests that students hate to take in school. I've scored tests for Ohio, Louisiana, Washington, Pennsylvania and Alaska. While doing this job in the spring and summer plus moving, I had little time left for writing.

I hope you enjoyed reading *JUDITH'S PLACE*. My husband and I visited Amish country last summer in Berlin, Ohio, so it was helpful in finishing writing Book Two in my Amish series. I asked Amish women various questions to make sure my understanding of their traditions and faith were accurate.

Recipes

In my Amish series, Samuel Weaver loves Rachel's butterscotch pie so I am including the recipe here for you to try. Something I learned while making the meringue is **never** use a plastic bowl or plastic beaters. I used both and the meringue never got stiff. When I used a stainless steel bowl and beaters, I had no problem with getting the meringue stiff. You could use cool whip in place of the meringue to save time and sprinkle butterscotch chips on the whipped topping.

Butterscotch Pie

¼ c. butter

2 tbsp. water

1 c. light brown sugar

1/4 c. corn starch

2 c. whole milk

pinch salt

3 large egg yolks (reserve egg whites for meringue)

½ tsp. vanilla

1 (9 inch) prepared (baked and cooled)

Preheat oven to 350°.

Beat egg yolks with 2 tbsp. sugar. Add 1/4 c. milk, corn starch, salt. Whisk together.

In a sauce pan, cook water and sugar till sugar is melted. Bring to a boil and boil for 2 minutes. Add 1 3/4 c. milk. Bring to a boil.

Put a bit of hot milk in with the eggs.

Add egg mixture to sauce pan and cook on low/medium heat till thickened. Stirring constantly. Add butter and vanilla, and stir another minute.

Pour into your pre-baked pie shell.

Meringue

- 3 egg whites
- ½ tsp. vanilla
- ¼ tsp. cream of tartar
- 6 tbsp. sugar

With a mixer, beat egg whites, vanilla and cream of tartar till soft peaks form. Gradually add sugar, beating till stiff and glossy peaks form, and sugar is all dissolved. Spread meringue over slightly warm filling, sealing to edge of crust. Bake at 350° for 12-15 minutes or till meringue is golden. Cool.

Or you could make a graham cracker crust.

Carrot Cake

This recipe makes a 9 x 13 cake.

- 4 eggs
- 1 1/4 vegetable oil or canola oil
- 2 cups white sugar
- 2 teaspoons vanilla extract
- 2 cups flour
- 2 teaspoons baking soda
- 2 teaspoons baking powder
- 1/2 teaspoon salt
- 2 teaspoons cinnamon
- 3 cups grated carrots
- 1 cup chopped pecans (optional)

Frosting

- 1/2 cup butter (softened)
- 8 ounces of cream cheese (softened)
- 1 teaspoon vanilla extract
- 4 cups confectioners' sugar

Directions

Preheat oven to 350 degrees and grease and flour a 9 x 13 inch pan or use a cooking spray.

In a large bowl, beat together eggs, oil, white sugar and 2 teaspoons of vanilla. Mix in flour, baking soda, baking powder, salt and cinnamon. Stir in carrots. Fold in pecans. Pour into prepared pan.

Bake in the preheated oven for 40 to 50 minutes, or until a toothpick inserted into the center of the cake comes out clean.

Let cool in pan for 10 minutes, then turn out onto a wire rack and cool completely.

To Make Frosting: In a medium bowl, combine butter, cream cheese, confectioners' sugar and 1 teaspoon vanilla. Beat until the mixture is smooth and creamy. Frost the cooled cake.

A Sneak Peek of *Fleeting Hope*, Book Three of Dreams of Plain Daughters Series!

Chapter One

Ruth Yoder couldn't make her legs walk into the ICU hospital room. Memories flooded her brain. Eleven years ago she was in the same situation as her friend Judith was now. Seeing Judith sitting by her boyfriend, Jacob, broke her heart. Her fiancé Daniel also had been unconscious from a buggy accident. In another month they would've been married, but Daniel had died. He was the love of her life. Maybe she had loved him too much, and that was why God had taken Daniel away from her. Had she put Daniel first before her heavenly Father? She'd been caught up in wedding plans and thrilled about the new house Daniel had built for their new life together.

Staring at Judith's bowed head, she couldn't interrupt her. *I hope Judith's prayers are answered.* She'd prayed for Daniel to recover, but his internal injuries were too great for his body to overcome.

"She's been here all day beside him," a nurse said softly to her. "Maybe you can get her to take a break so she can get something to eat."

Ruth nodded. "That's a good suggestion. We teach together in our Amish school."

"She looks too young to be a teacher."

"She's eighteen and our teachers are allowed to start..." her voice trailed off when she saw Judith glance at her.

"Ruth, *danki* for coming," Judith said as she walked toward her.

When Judith was next to her, Ruth saw tears in her blue eyes. She gave Judith a big hug and said, "I want to be here for you."

The nurse looked at Judith. "Why don't you take a break and get something to eat while I chart Jacob's vital signs?"

"Thank you, Sue. I'm glad you're his nurse. You've been wonderful. I do need to get out of here and stretch my legs." Judith moved so the nurse could enter the ICU room. "Ruth, let's go to the cafeteria. I need to talk to you."

I wonder if Judith wants to take time off from teaching so she can be here. Ruth knew Jacob and Judith had gotten close in the short time they had courted. "That sounds *gut* to me."

"I hope Jacob wakes up soon." From the doorway, Judith watched Jacob for a moment.

"He has a lot of people praying that he will."

"We can take the elevator," Judith said. "I know where the cafeteria is. I had a cup of coffee with Martha and Robert yesterday."

"This has to be hard on them too."

"*Ya.* The whole Weaver family were here all day yesterday excerpt Samuel left to feed their livestock."

Ruth followed Judith into the elevator and watched her push the button for the cafeteria floor. "If you want company, I can stay with you the whole afternoon. My driver went shopping, so she isn't in any hurry to return to Fields Corner."

Judith squeezed Ruth's hand. "I'd like for you to stay. The Weavers are coming back this evening. I'll ride back to Fields Corner with them."

Once they were in the cafeteria, Ruth said, "I already had lunch but I think I'll get dessert. This cafeteria is huge."

Judith nodded. "When the ambulance got to Jacob, they realized he needed to be transported to a hospital with a trauma center. The University of Cincinnati Medical Center is the only one in our area with an adult level one trauma center."

I won't tell Judith that Daniel died here. It definitely won't help her to know it was the same hospital that they decided was the best one for Daniel. After picking up a tray, Ruth selected a slice of cherry pie. She removed a cup and filled it with coffee. She waited until Judith made her selection before paying the cashier for both of them.

"Let me pay you back for my food," Judith said.

Ruth shook her head. "It's my treat. I'm glad you decided to eat something."

After they were seated at a small table, Ruth bowed her head to pray silently. *Dear Father, please spare Judith the pain I went through after losing Daniel. Heal Jacob of his injuries so he will survive from his terrible accident. I give thanks that he's still alive and danki that Judith wasn't in the buggy. She's like a daughter to me. In Jesus' Name, I pray. Amen.*

Judith said, "I have so much to tell you, but wish it were under different circumstances."

What could it be? Did Jacob and Judith talk about getting married, Ruth wondered.

"Jacob told me he loved me a month ago. He wanted to court me before, but I never went to any of the Sunday singings. I hate to mention my cell phone, because I know we aren't supposed to use them...but we've enjoyed talking on the phone this winter. It helped to get to know each other even better. But we're going to stop using the phones to talk each night because we both want to get baptized this year. I talked to Bishop Amos about taking instructions. And Jacob already did too."

"That's *wunderbaar*."

Judith grinned. "What's *wunderbaar*? That Jacob told me he loved me or that we're getting baptized?"

"All of it is. I'm happy for you both. I'm sure the school board will be happy to hear that you're getting baptized." Ruth smiled.

"Bishop Amos was definitely pleased." Judith took a spoonful of her soup. "I didn't think I could eat anything but this broccoli soup is delicious."

Ruth took a sip of her coffee. "I'm sorry I complained about you getting your GED. I'm proud of you for accomplishing your goal, but have to admit I'm relieved you're staying here to teach."

"I love teaching with you in our school." Judith exhaled a deep breath. "I'm not sure what will happen now. When Jacob comes out of the coma, he'll be upset that he has a broken leg and arm. He just bought forty acres from Seth Graber. Jacob wanted the farm for us when we get married."

"Did he have to get a bank loan?" Ruth asked.

"No he didn't get it from the bank, but his *dat* loaned him the amount he didn't have. He'll want to plant soon but he won't be able to now with his injuries."

"Well, it's still just March but I bet Samuel and their *dat* would plant the fields for Jacob. I'm sure he'll have therapy after the casts come off, but could still be able to do the farm work this summer."

"If he comes out of the coma."

"The accident just happened yesterday. And he survived it so that's a blessing."

"The doctor was vague. Each patient is different he said." Judith looked sad. "His head injury worries me, too, because he has a big knot on his forehead. Jacob must have hit his head hard."